The Annals of the Time Beyond Time

Volume I

Thomas R. Skidmore

SKYWATCHER

(a novel of the Time Beyond Time)

NOTE ON TEXT

This is a revised and expanded edition of the original 2010 text. Punctuation, wording, and formatting reflect these changes.

"Sadly now your thoughts turn to the stars; where we have gone you know you never can go.

Watcher of the skies, watcher of all, this is your fate alone, this fate is your own."

Peter Gabriel and Tony Banks, "Watcher of the Skies" from **Foxtrot**, 1972

CHAPTER ONE

It was a night, and event, that I'll never, *ever* forget. And it all started with the matter of my name, given to me by my mother, if not both she and my father.

And what's my name, you ask?

Well . . . if you promise not to laugh, I'll tell you.

It's an unusual name, to start with. See, my mother, and *her* mother, and her *mother's* mother are all from an alien race of winged women guardian warriors. My father, of course with him being an Earthman, had really nothing to do with how I was to be called. But I've gotta love him anyway. So what's my name, I hear you screaming?

Okay, okay . . .I'll tell you. My name's Skywatcher Hackett. My mom's name is Sunleaf Hackett. And my dad is named Steve Hackett.

(Yeah, you heard it right. That's for all you old-time Genesis fans reading this.)

All right, I can hear you shout, "C'mon, get on with it, will ya, HUH?" If you please, allow me this one little luxury of telling my story in my way. That's all I ask for now. Oh, before I get too involved in this adventure, I ought to inform you that -- well, I'll tell you during the course of the story. Okay with you?

Anyway, I was at home waiting for my dad to come home from work at the Foxtrot Time Works, where he's a top-notch supervisor. It's his job to see that the machines needed to maintain the flow of the Temporal Balance stay in good working order. Otherwise, there'd be the dreaded *Chaos* that everybody fears . . . and for good reason, too. See, what my daddy told me is that the Temporal Balance is needed to achieve total harmony with the Universe. In other words, every single thing in our Unverse has to be "just so."

If it isn't, well -- let's just say it isn't pretty to see, much less talk about.

I'm boring you so far, aren't I?

I promise it'll get a lot more exciting, so please stick with me on this.

It was somewhat late when my dad got home from work at the factory. He just put in a long shift, and boy, was he fit to be tied. And when my dad is tired, he could become irascible and grouchy. Kinda like good ol' Archie Bunker, only my dad's a lot nicer. Better looking, too.

He made his way to our kitchen, stopping at the refrigerator.

"Hey, Sunleaf, where's the diet cola?" he asked, in his inborn British accent.

"I'm sorry, I didn't get to the store. I was running around all over town on at least twenty-five different errands and I just couldn't --" called out Mom.

That made Dad really peeved. He didn't like not talking to Mom face-to-face. "Sunleaf, you know I can't speak to you when you're in another country. Get in the kitchen, will you?"

Instantly Mom literally flew into the kitchen, landing directly on his toes. She quickly pecked him on the cheek. He grimaced in pain. But he kept his cool about it.

"Where's Skywatcher at?" asked Dad.

"Oh, she's outside staring at the stars. It sort of fits her, you know. More or less," she replied.

"Well, I hope she realizes that I'm home and it's time for supper. By the way, what *are* we having, I ask, assuming we have *some* food about here."

"Well, Steve, it's like I finished telling you. I didn't get to the store and -- "

"Never mind that for now. Get Skywatcher in here, please."

Mom called out, loud as she could, "SKYWATCHER!! DADDY'S HOME!!"

When she did that routine she sounds just like your Edith Bunker, only a lot younger.

Quickly I stepped, or, if you will, *flew* in, hugging the stuffings out of Dad. I'm always glad to have him here with us. It makes me feel all giddy inside. "Hi, Daddy!" I squealed loudly into his ear, still giddy. His ears rang in pain. He hates it when I do that.

Of course, we talked about our day and how it went, what to eat for supper, etc. Yessiree, we were a typically happy family in spite of it all.

Little did I know that my gladness and joy wouldn't last all much longer.

CHAPTER TWO

After we ate our dinner (which consisted mainly of leftovers), I went back outside.

"Where are you off to, little lady?" asked Dad rather grouchily.

"Oh, just outside to look at the sky and stars some more, if that's okay," I said.

"Well, don't be too long. It's getting quite late in the evening."

"And Skywatcher, be careful, okay, sweetie?" added Mom.

"Okay," I said. And I literally flew out the door. Once again I felt all giddy. For now,

at that rate in, if you'll pardon the expression, time.

Later that evening I was sitting on the grassy knoll outside our house, just minding my own

business, as is usually the case, when I felt a cool, gradual breeze coming from the eastern part of

the sky.

I didn't mind it at first. In fact, it was rather refreshing. But then it intensified in strength,

almost knocking me off my feet. Boy oh boy, was I in for a real surprise!! You see, the sudden breeze actually caused a small group of clouds to form a shape of some kind, although I didn't know exactly what. But it was a very . . . *lovely* sight to see. It's almost like it was forming a -- *person* or something.

Soon I found out what kind of person-shape it would be.

It was a -- *woman!!* With long black hair, and huge wings. She almost looked like my mother, in a relative sense. She was really pretty, too. Then I heard what sounded like a roar of thunder . . . and it was calling out my name.

"Skywatcher . . . Skywatcher . . . hear me," it -- or rather, *she* said.

I don't mind telling you I got really nervous when I heard the sky actually call my name out loud like that. In fact, I was downright *scared!!*

"Skywatcher . . . Skywatcher . . . hear me calling out to you."

Out of my growing curiosity, I finally turned around to look, listen, and respond. I don't know *why* I responded, though.

"What do you want?" I asked.

"Skywatcher . . . I am pleased that you have responded. You have been chosen by the Deaconesses of our race."

"Chosen to do what?"

"You've been chosen to aid your Realm in the times ahead of you, young one. And I do not mind telling you the times will be perilous -- for all concerned, including our people and your family. So heed my prophecy very carefully." She sounded really scared.

"Okay," I said, "I'll listen."

The nice lady in the sky sighed in relief and then continued talking.

"First off, allow me to introduce myself. I am Moon Swan, your maternal ancestor. I have been sent by the Lords of the Temporal Balance to inform you of the quest you are to undertake. As I said, it's quite perilous. That is why even now I fear for your safety, my special one. Indeed, my heart is doubtless pained for you."

"If you're so worried about me, then why did they send you to tell me about this -- *quest* I have to go on?" I queried.

Moon Swan looked like she was going to cry.

"Oh, how I grieve for your well-being, young Skywatcher. You have so much to learn -- and yet so little time to accomplish it in." I could almost actually *feel* her tears. That's when I got *really* scared.

"I fear I cannot reveal any more at this time, young Skywatcher, but suffice it to say again you, your family, and your world are in peril. Go to your leader as soon as you can, and inform him of this news. And if you must, you may *reveal this prophecy to your parents. They are good people, and they will no doubt support you."*

"That's nice to know, but my dad won't believe any of this," I said to her.

I saw a slight smile on Moon Swan's face. She looked even prettier with her smile.

"Oh, I'll make *him believe it, whether he chooses to or not."*

And with that, Moon Swan faded back into the sky, but not before she said her last words -- for the moment, anyhow.

"We shall see each other again, young Skywatcher. And be brave for us all . . ."

CHAPTER THREE

That moment I flew back into the house, shaking all over. I *had* to tell my folks.

"Mom! Dad!! Guess what I saw in the sky just a little bit ago?"

As usual, Dad was his gruff, British self.

"Let me see . . . you saw stars and birds and clouds."

"I saw a lot more than those, Dad." I turned my eyes to Mom. "Mom," I asked, "do you know someone named Moon Swan?"

Mom looked at me with a funny expression on her face. It wasn't too pleasant.

"What did you just say?" she asked rather icily.

"Do you know someone named Moon Swan? That's all I asked."

No one uttered a word for several minutes.

"You listen to me right now, young lady. I do *not* want that name mentioned in this house ever again. That name's nothing but trouble for our people. That's the end of it," said Mom angrily.

Out of curiosity, Dad turned to Mom.

"Why is it that you don't want that name mentioned?" he asked.

Mom sighed very heavily and testily.

"Steve, it's a long story, and I really have no desire to go through all of that nonsense again, if that's all right with you." Then she turned back to me, still angry. "As for you, young lady, if you *ever* say that woman's name again, I'll personally wash your mouth out with every bar of soap we have. Is that clear?!" She paused. "Now," she said to me some more, "you get ready for bed. Move."

I turned back to Dad, hoping for some relief. I wouldn't get any.

"You best do what your mother says. No need for any more grief," he said.

Wearily, I went up to my bedroom, having said good night somewhat weakly.

After I got into my bed, I heard the sounds of my parents arguing. That it was about me I had no

doubt. Lords of the Balance, I hate their arguing. Makes me want to throw up my cookies.

Soon I fell asleep.

And *that's* when Moon Swan kept her promise.

CHAPTER FOUR

It was in my dreams that I saw her again. Her voice called out loud and strong.

"Skywatcher . . . Skywatcher . . . hear me, and respond."

Quickly I yelled out to her.

"Here I am."

Swiftly she flew and landed right near where I stood. She didn't look any happier.

"It is good to see you again, young Skywatcher. But I fear my joy in your presence is to be short-lived. There is so much more that I must reveal to you, and doubtless it is not pleasant to describe. But it must be so that you'd be aware of the peril you're now in."

"What is this -- *peril* you keep mentioning" I asked her.

"I can only answer that if you feel that you're brave enough to handle such grim truths. I don't speak of this lightly, and you mustn't take it as such. Am I understood on this matter?"

Slowly I nodded my head. I got the message.

Moon Swan, for the first time, actually *smiled* at me. It wasn't to be a long smile.

"Now, young one, prepare yourself for what I'm about to tell you." She paused sadly then eyed me very intently, as if there were lasers going through me. I became really scared by this point.

"Heed my words very carefully, young Skywatcher. As I'm sure you know, there are Realms beyond our own. These are held in the flow of the Temporal Balance by the Fates of Time. Their task is to maintain overall harmony for all the Noble Beings, of which you are one, Skywatcher. Yet even now there are those who seek to disrupt the total Balance, bringing about Chaos, Anarchy, and Destruction. Those who wish this are planning a massive invasion so totally devastating none will survive. Not even you, my young emissary." Moon Swan grew even sadder, although her face didn't show it.

"If what you're telling me is true," I said, " then how can I stop this from happening?" The fear in my voice was clearly felt by Moon Swan.

"Oh, you'll just know, that's all. Now, have you told your parents about me?"

"Yeah, I told them. Like you said, my dad didn't believe it. But my mom got really mad when I told her about you. She said that if I mentioned your name again, she was going to wash my mouth out with every bar of soap we have in the house. Why?"

Moon Swan paused a long time before answering.

"It's a rather long story, but on our home world I was one of the Chief Prophetesses of our tribe. It was my task to interpret every sign I would come into contact with. And I did this task with the utmost efficiency. That is, until I saw the One Sign that I was never to see or divulge, lest it bring disaster to our people...and to every Realm in the entire Universe of the Time Beyond Time."

"And *did* you reveal what the signs showed?" I asked.

"I most certainly did, Skywatcher. And I don't need to tell you our people weren't too happy about.it. Some accused me of being insane -- and that was being kind on their part. Others, no doubt, wanted me punished. Or worse."

I know I didn't need to ask what this prophecy was, but I did so anyway.

"And, uh, what *was* this prophecy that caused our people to want you to eat soap, among other things?"

Moon Swan then gave me a really pained look.

"It is . . . this very prophecy I'm giving you right now." Then the tears rolled down her face, and I felt really bad for her by this point in our conversation.

"Do you really mean to say that I *have* to go on this quest?" I queried.

Moon Swan drew closer to me, holding my face in her hand. She was still crying.

"Oh, Skywatcher. You have no idea how much I grieve for you. You are a mere child of thirteen, it is known, but inside you is the very thing needed to save our Realm from the imminent danger about to overtake us all. But I wish you to know that I will be with you and your family, in spirit, all the way through this ordeal." Then she kissed me on my forehead, stroking my hair gently. Her smile seemed to return.

"I love you so very much . . . my beautiful Skywatcher," said Moon Swan, hugging me. *"And now I'm going to see your old man and make him face the truth about everything . . . "*

And with that, everything faded away . . .

CHAPTER FIVE

I woke up, shouting for my parents. Instantly they raced in with my dad ahead as usual. They didn't look too happy.

"What is it, Skywatcher?" Dad asked. Mom remained quiet.

"Dad!! Mom!! I saw Moon Swan, in my dreams. She said that -- " I began.

"Stop it right now, young lady!!" screeched Mom. "I told you not to mention her name again. Steve," she said, turning to Dad, "get the soap out of the bathroom."

"Get it yourself, Sunleaf. I'm going to the kitchen. I'm hungry," said Dad.

A few minutes later I heard Dad rummaging in the refrigerator. When my dad gets hungry late at night -- especially if he gets woken up for no reason -- he likes to eat a turkey lunch meat sandwich. He says it soothes his itchy nerves.

What he ended up with was a lot more than turkey. He can tell you himself . . .

From the words of Mr. Steve Hackett himself:

Like my daughter said to you earlier, I was foraging about in the fridge, prepping my sandwich when out of the clear blue, or black, as the case may be, I caught a strange light peeking out from behind me . . . along with an even stranger voice.

"Hello, Stephen. I wish to speak with you," the odd, yet clearly female voice called.

I turned around, and saw someone whom I thought was Sunleaf, playing a late-night prank. A prank which I was undoubtedly and emphatically *not* in the mood for.

"Sunleaf, what are you doing down here?" I asked rather perturbedly.

"I am not my descendant, Stephen. I am Moon Swan. I'm sure your daughter told you about me." She appeared rather confident in her delusional idea. But I wasn't buying it. Not by a long shot.

I continued to eat my sandwich, not paying her any mind. Then she grew agressively angry, drawing herself to my position.

"Put down that sandwich, you meathead, and listen up!" she yelled, grabbing my sandwich right smack out of my mouth. I, of course, managed to get one last gulp of my late, lamented snack.

"What do you want of me?" I asked the strange woman.

Her gaze did not elicit any type of friendly response whatsoever. I might have known, knowing the kind of family that I somehow married into. A real bunch of weirdos is all I can say . . . for now, at that rate.

"You didn't answer my question, Miss, uh . . . Moon Swan, was it?" I stated.

She gave me that same icy-cold gaze, shaking her head in severe anger.

"I came here to tell you about the danger your young daughter is in, and you get all huffy with me. And this from a guy who would rather be romantically intimate with a sandwich *than be worried sick about his child. Oh, Stephen, Stephen, Stephen,"* she finally said. It was still in no friendly tone of voice.

Feeling equally unsympathetic, I retorted out to her face, as lovely as it was.

"Well, at least you got my name right."

"Look, for now let's end this childish argument. As I tried to tell you ere I was so crassly interrupted, you're all in grave peril. I know for a fact that Skywatcher tried to inform you, but naturally, in your case, you decided to ignore it. And that ticks me off to no end."

"Is it my fault that my daughter has an over-active imagination?"

Moon Swan remained quite angered for a long stint of time.

"I'm not going to argue with you any longer, Stephen. All I can say is that you best see your elected official ASAP. Your entire Realm is in grave danger from the Forces that are too powerful to contain in the proper flows of the Temporal Balance. I hope to the Fates you can at least pretend *to understand this."*

Drawing a heavy sigh, I reluctantly decided to listen. After all, I wasn't doing much else now, was I?

Within a few minutes I found myself growing quite interested in Moon Swan's rather wild tale concerning my kid, even though I, myself, wasn't all that keen on believing her at that point. And, as is my nature, I said so.

"So what you're saying to me is that my kid has to help fulfill this daffy prophecy of your women-folk that got her in a panic, and you in hot water. What kind of invasion are we discussing here?" I questioned.

"I find your lack of awareness to be excruciatingly aggravating. It's also giving me a headache.

But suffice it to say that it's an all-out, massive armed attack from those who hail from the Nether

Realms of Unknown Space and Time. There'll be terrible wars, devastation, and panic . . . unless

you get yourselves to see your elected head official now!!!"

Without fail, I made my way to Skywatcher's bedroom.

CHAPTER SIX

From Skywatcher's diary:

A loud knock woke me up from a little cat-nap I was taking.

"Skywatcher, wake up. Now." It was Dad calling out to me. Quickly I opened the door.

"What is it, Dad?" I asked.

"Get dressed. Right now. We're going out. You, your mother, and I are going to see 'King' Weigndin. We have to warn him about this whole mad thing due to happen."

"Wow!! You mean we get to finally meet King Wingy-Ding?" I squeaked out.

"Just get dressed, huh? I'll get that mother of yours ready as well."

I had to admit that the idea of meeting our head official was kinda neat. My dad, of course, didn't see it that way. Why, I don't know.

At least, not yet anyway…

An hour later, we were on our way to see King Wingy-Ding himself.

I only hope he takes us seriously, though I knew he'd think otherwise…

From Sunleaf's words:

I don't know about you, but I clearly *wasn't* happy with the way things were going at that stage. First that daughter of mine tells me this nutty "prophecy" given to her by my so-called "great" maternal ancestor, which *really* angered me to no end, but then that husband of mine gets me out of bed to see our alleged "leader" whom I have absolutely no desire to meet, much less talk to. And now we're on our way to who-knows-where.

There are times when it just doesn't pay to get out of bed for the day, and this was one of those times. We all can thank my daughter for this little epic saga. I was really beginning to hate my life at this point in the game.

But that's enough about my personal troubles. On with the story, nonsensical such as it is, at any rate.

After we all got ourselves dressed, we left the house and set off on this madcap quest to see King Wingy-Ding and somehow *try* to tell him of some insane "prophecy of doom" that my kid somehow heard about, even though I felt it was the biggest waste of, if you'll excuse the term, time in the history of the entire Realm.

One-third of the way into our trip, I turned to Skywatcher.

"I sure hope to the Fates that you're satisfied, young lady!" I snarled.

"Mom, don't you see? I *have* to do this. It's for all our good," she said tensely.

"Oh, Skywatcher, you don't '*have*' to do every little thing that people tell you.

Did you ever hear of the word 'no'? Or doesn't that register with this 'prophetic vision' that Moon Swan gave you?"

And then she did something I didn't like: she gave me a hard look that said, in effect, "Go to the Realms of Mud with that remark."

"Don't you *ever* give that look again, young woman!! Is that clear?!?"

"Mom, you can yell at me all you want, but I'm not backing down from this," she said in that defiant tone. Wearily, I resigned myself to that fact. Glancing sideways at my husband, I hissed, "This is all *your* fault. I can't believe that I actually married you."

Steve clenched his jaw tight, trying his tiniest best not to say anything that he'd regret. My mother was right. I shouldn't have married an Earthman. They're trouble, she said. But did I listen?

No. And now I'm stuck with it all.

Okay, okay . . . back to our story.

Within an hour we arrived at the home/office of our duly-elected mayor, the so-called 'King' Weigndin, alias Wingy-Ding. I was definitely *not* looking forward to this at all.

Casually, Steve knocked on the door. Instantly it opened, and we were met by a tallish guy with short dark hair and grey eyes. He was decked up like a pianist, and he also wasn't too happy to see us. And he said so, in a slightly high-pitched voice.

"What's the idea of coming here at this time of night?" he asked tersely.

Before I could stop her, Skywatcher rapidly made her point be known.

"We're here to see King Wingy-Ding, I mean 'King' Weigndin on a matter of grave importance," she said. Inwardly I groaned, while Steve said not one word as of yet.

Evidently the doorman-dressed-as-pianist wasn't too impressed.

"Look, he's asleep. Couldn't this wait till morning?"

"No," said Skywatcher.

"What do you mean, 'no'?" asked the doorman, looking at Skywatcher.

"It's important that we see him. This Realm, and all the others are in terrible danger. We've *got* to see him!" *That* seemed to get his attention.

"Oh, all right. Come on in," he said.

In a few seconds we were shown in.

CHAPTER SEVEN

From Skywatcher's diary:

The inside of King Wingy-Ding's place was - how should I put it? -- radiantly

sloppy. I mean, there was gold lace strewn out all over the floor, silver plates that look like no

one bothered to wash them, and diamond floors so caked with fried chicken grease you could

play ice hockey on them. But we weren't here to be his housekeepers. Our mission was more

important. I just hope that King Wingy-Ding understands that—for *his* sake as well as our own.

Immediately the doorman went up a semi-cleaned flight of steps, making some kind of knocking

noise, shouting the mayor's name at the same time. In a few moments he returned downstairs and

made his way back to us. He still wasn't too happy about any of this, even though he kept his

even temper about it all.

"He should be down here in a few minutes. Try to make yourselves at home, within reason," he

said flatly. "And if you need anything, just ask for Tony -- that's my name, in case you were

wondering."

"Okay, thank you, Mr. Tony," I said.

That got him a little smile.

"Uh, no, no, it's just Tony," he replied, chuckling. Then he left us.

Nervously we waited, looking at each other in disbelief. Naturally, Mom was still awfully ticked at me for dragging all of us into this adventure. Dad, on the other hand, kept a surprisingly even temper about it.

"I'm warning you, young lady, if this is one of your wild flights of fancy -- "hissed Mom sternly.

"Mom," I replied, "how many times do I have to try to convince you this is the real deal. Moon Swan wouldn't lie to me, would she?" She didn't say much after that.

Next it was Dad's turn to question me.

"Just how did you find yourself mixed up in all of this?"

I paused a moment before answering.

"You know something? I honestly don't know."

"Well . . . that's good enough for me," he said.

"It sure isn't good enough for *me*, young lady!!" said Mom, still mad.

After the few minutes elapsed, Tony returned to the main room where we were at now. He cleared his throat very loudly.

"All hail our duly-elected official, the illustrious 'King' Weigndin," he declared formally. Out of respect, we bowed down.

Seconds later, we stood back up, and gazed upon King Wingy-Ding. He was a slightly dumpy-looking guy, totally bald with blue eyes, and a silly smile emanating from his face. On his head he wore what looked like a KFC fried chicken bucket decorated with baubles that more than resembled stale buttermilk biscuits. He was clad in a gaudy bathrobe that looked as if it hadn't been dry-cleaned in eons. At least he *smelled* clean, at any rate.

Tony turned to King Wingy-Ding, announcing us as guests.

"Nests? Sure, there's nests," said King Wingy-Ding.

We couldn't believe our ears!! Hastily, Tony turned to us.

"I should've mentioned that 'King' Weigndin is a little on the hard-of-hearing side," he hissed quietly.

Now he tells us. Oh well.

I made my way to the leader.

"Your majesty, I'd like to speak to you, if you please -- " I began.

"Sneeze? No, little darling, don't have to sneeze. Don't have any allergies."

"Please, your majesty, we're all in grave danger."

"Manger? It's not Christmastime. It's a bit too early in the year for that."

Evidently this was getting us nowhere.

That's when my Dad *really* let loose.

"Now look, you," he said, "you'd best listen to my daughter."

"Huh?? Water? Well, I *am* thirsty," said King Wingy-Ding.

We all looked at each other, thinking that this guy's nuts.

A bad thought entered my mind by now: *No one's believing me . . .*

My Dad was about ready to lose it, but fortunately my Mom stepped in.

"Look, Steve, there's no point becoming angry now," she said.

"No, *you* look, Sunleaf! This is *partially* your fault, too. I mean, she *is* descended from your people," he retorted back.

Now Mom *really* got mad at my Dad.

"Oh sure!! Blame it all on *me*, why don't you?!! If you weren't such a hardhead -- " Little did we know that King Wingy-Ding was within, if you'll pardon the saying, earshot of their conversation.

"What? Party? Okay, right, let's *party*!!" he yelled. And let me tell you, when he wants a party he gets it . . . like it or not.

And so the festivities started, in spite of my trying to warn everyone of the danger now growing all around . . .

CHAPTER EIGHT

The party lasted for more than an hour, with guests popping in and out like wildfire. We were definitely not too happy about the situation as it was. During the course of the whole thing King Wingy-Ding announced that the gala would last all night.

My Dad had to shout above the noise just to try to make himself heard.

"Excuse me, but I think it's high time for this little shindig to end," he said.

"What's that? Friend? Sure, you're my friend. Everybody's my friend," shouted back King Wingy-Ding. "Let's all sing a song!!" Instantly the crowd, which grew in number, yelled their approval . . . as if it was really needed.

"Okay, Tony...*hit it!!*" called out King Wingy-Ding.

Immediately Tony made his way to the oddly immaculate piano, striking up a melody that only King Wingy-Ding knew from the top of his head. The three of us looked at each other in disgust. How do we put an end to all this?

As expected, King Wingy-Ding got up off the throne, did a little dance, opened his mouth and started to sing:

"Just as I thought it was going all right, I found out I'm wrong when I thought I was right;

Always the same, it's just a shame, that's all..."

(Phil Collins, "That's All" from **Genesis**, 1983)

Then suddenly my Dad was hit by an idea. He made a hand signal to Tony, who unfortunately couldn't respond, as he was in the middle of playing his piano. Impatiently Dad waited until King Wingy-Ding stopped singing.

Quickly he walked up to Tony, who was still at the piano. He whispered in Tony's ear. Tony nodded, then left the piano.

Then Dad signaled to Mom and I, and we rushed up to them.

"Remember when Tony said that our alleged 'leader' was a little deaf?" asked Dad to me.

"Yeah, sure I remember," I said, nodding my head.

"Well . . . I may be able to help you to convince him of the danger that you're so fond of warning us about." And for the first time in a long while, Dad actually smiled at me.

An instant ot two later my Dad waltzed up to King Wingy-Ding.

"Uh, sir, if I may say, that's a nice bird," said Dad.

"What's that? A word? Sure, you can have a word," replied King Wingy-Ding. He was all smiles . . . for now.

My Dad's plan was in full motion!

CHAPTER NINE

From Mr. Steve Hackett's words:

I had this rather daffy idea in my head. Having found out about our leader's hearing problem I thought, for my kid's benefit, to exploit it to some good use, in spite of its total implausibilty. And, unbelievably, it seemed to be working.

I can only hope that he'd get the message in regards to Skywatcher's given prophetic vision. But if you'll excuse the words, only time would tell…

"Uh, sire, if I may, your helm's a manger," I said.

King Wingy-Ding paused, now quite tense.

"What's that? Did you say the Realm's in danger?" he asked.

We all nodded our heads somberly.

"Oh, well, that's -- THE REALM'S IN DANGER?!!?" Now he panicked. "Get the Royal Guardian Army!! Arm the troops!! *GET THIS MESS CLEANED UP!!*"

In a minute or so we were met by the Captain of the Royal Guardian Army. He was a tall man, with grey-blue eyes, long sandy-blond hair, and a slightly greyish beard. He wore the traditional soldier's garb, complete with a medium-length cloak. At his side sat a laser-staff. Overall, he looked quite imposing, almost intimidating. That sense disappeared when he smiled slightly.

"My men will be alert and ready for just about anything, Mr. Hackett," he said. "Oh, incidentally, what is it that we had to prepare for?"

I didn't want to answer him, but out of my love for my daughter, I did so anyway. Just out of courtesy, I figured.

"My daughter here," I replied, pointing at Skywatcher, "received a 'vision' of impending doom on our entire Realm from some invading army out of the Unknown Realms of Space and Time."

Oddly, his face blenched, as if a dark fear struck him. Still it didn't faze him . . . too much.

"We'll be ready for them," he said. "Oh, by the way, I'm Captain M. Ruther. And I can assure you that we'll all be safe and ready." He patted my shoulder in confidence.

My own thoughts did not echo that vow.

CHAPTER TEN

From Skywatcher's diary:

An hour after the party was quickly stopped, and the army prepared to do battle, the three of us bade a hasty farewell to King Wingy-Ding and his gang of bananas. Then we fled out out the palace.

My Mom was still irritated at me for waking her up in the middle of the night and dragging us all the way over here. And she said so, in no uncertain terms.

"Just you wait until we get home, young woman!" hissed Mom.

"*If* we get home," I said back to her.

"What do you mean by that?" asked Dad.

I didn't get a chance to reply, because at that exact moment we were met by the same bright light that got us here in the first place. We then turned around and saw -- *Moon Swan*, standing in front of us. She looked as pretty as ever.

My Mom made a nasty face at her. Clearly you can tell they didn't get along.

"Well, well, well. My 'illustrious' ancestor," she said sarcastically. "What have you done to my kid?!!"

"Hey, she's my kid, too, Sunleaf!" yelled Moon Swan back at Mom.

"Really?!! Who died and let *you* give birth to her?!?"

Moon Swan remained ticked off.

"Listen, my blood is in her, too, you know. All our people's blood is in her. Or did you forget that after you married this *guy?"* said Moon Swan, pointing at my Dad. He really was not a happy camper at that stage. And he decided to do something about it.

"Look, ladies, could we put this cheap alien soap opera aside for now?"

Reluctantly, Moon Swan and my Mom did so . . . for now.

"Do whatever you want, Moon Swan," said Mom wearily.

Instantly Moon Swan placed her hand on my forehead.

"Now close your eyes, Skywatcher, and focus on the words and visions that I'm about to give you. Concentrate . . . concentrate . . . and see the ones who wish on us great harm."

I did so, and what I saw scared me to death.

"What do you see?" asked Moon Swan.

"I see . . . a giant airship from out of nowhere, making their way to -- *the Foxtrot Time Works!!* They're going to destroy it! DADDY!! DADDY!!!" I screamed.

My parents raced up to me. I was shaking all over.

"What is it, love? What's wrong?" asked Dad, worried with fear.

"Dad, please don't go to work in the morning! *Please!*" I pleaded.

An odd look crossed my Dad's face.

"You know I can't afford to -- oh, I get it now. You saw in your mind that I was in danger, and you're trying to protect me," he said.

"That's only half of it, Stephen. The Foxtrot Time Works is, of course, where you're employed, but it's also the grand prize sought out by the forces of the Hyradian Empire. They're *the ones who want all-out Chaos, Anarchy, and Destruction. And I dare say, Skywatcher's the only hope we have."* She then turned to me. *"I must warn you, though, not to take them lightly. They may act like a bunch of ill-brained, comedic, idiotic rejects at times, but their intentions are quite sinister and evil. So be on your guard, my young Skywatcher . . . and be always brave for us all."*

I didn't need to be reminded twice. And I think my parents finally got the message -- well, my Dad was more convinced than Mom was.

"Well, love," said Dad, "now I can honestly say that I actually *believe* what you've just made us experience. *And* I can also now say that, to be quite frank, I'm now scared to death for your well-being." He turned to my Mom. "Isn't that right, Sunleaf?"

"Oh, I suppose so, Steve. I suppose so," was all Mom said at that point.

Moon Swan turned to my Dad again.

"At last, I've finally convinced you, Stephen. Now, Sunleaf," said Moon Swan, *"are* you *convinced? Or do I have to ram it in your face again and again until you understand?"*

Mom wearily nodded her head in agreement. She turned to me.

"You better come through for us all, young lady. If you don't, you'll be the sorriest

Startian/human hybrid girl in the entire Realm. I do hope I'm clear on this."

"For the last time, Sunleaf, stop picking on our daughter!! I've had quite enough of this for one

lifetime, and it's time to end your little grudge forever -- *for our child's sake!!* Is *THAT* clear?!"

boomed out Dad. Boy, was he mad!

"That will do, Stephen," interrupted Moon Swan. *"Your daughter's quest must begin first thing*

in the morning. Now go and get some sleep. Skywatcher will need all her true strength and

Startia-bred agility for her mission."

And *that* was the last good night I would ever see . . .

CHAPTER ELEVEN

"Judge not this race by empty remains; do you judge God by his creatures when they are dead?

For now, the lizard's shed its tail; this is the end of Man's long union with Earth..."

Peter Gabriel & Tony Banks, "Watcher of the Skies" from **Foxtrot**, 1972

From the Log of Robrack, commander of the Hyradian Forces:

When I first laid out our plans of taking, by force, the glittering prize that is the Foxtrot Time

Works I, of course, was met with a great deal of skepticism. I mean, that isn't just *any* prize we

were to seize. Not by any means. The legend was that whoever controlled the Time Works would

rule the entire Realm of the Time Beyond Time.

(Sounds ambitious for a bunch of us so-called "glorified pirates," doesn't it?)

Anyway, throughout the passing weeks, a sense of electric excitement was in the air. I had to

admit, it *was* a tantalizing prospect. If all went well, it would definitely be our time to shine. I

tried, naturally, to keep a even demeanor about the whole affair.

(Of course, there *are* some things -- well, that *one* thing I didn't plan on. And that was that flying

brat named -- oh, I can't remember her name now. Skywatcher, that's it. Ooh, I hate that kid.

Then again, I wasn't there to win any popularity contests. But I'm digressing here, aren't I?)

Where was I? Hmmm . . . oh yeah. The attack on the Foxtrot Time Works.

The morning that our attack was to commence, our electric excitement increased a hundred-fold. It was deathly quiet for most of the time. No one even ate that morning. The anticipation was enough to get us going.

And then -- *zero hour!!*

Frenzily I shouted out to my troops.

"Men, this is it!! Our moment in the sun is here!! Now let's go out and take it all!! No prisoners!! No mercy is to be shown to anyone!! If people get hurt, that's not our concern!! Only our grand prize will we show any feeling for!! Now -- *we STRIKE!!!*"

The boys roared in delight. They knew.

In a matter of hours we boarded our highly-advanced airship, armed with the best weaponry we had. I was the first on board our mighty ship, which I personally named *Sky Skull One*. With me was my adviser, a slightly dumpy, grey-haired guy who always seemed easy-going . . . in fact a little *too* easy-going, I thought.

Soon afterwards we took flight. Nothing—and I mean, *nothing* was to stand in our way. (Or so we thought.)

From Skywatcher's diary:

I have to tell you right now, seeing the vision of that giant airship, with those powerful weapons, really gave me the creeps.

"Now you know your opponent in this, our darkest hour. I trust you to find some way to stop them," said Moon Swan. She had that same sad look on her face.

My Mom and Dad grew very worried. Scared, even.

"But how will she know what to do?" asked my Dad.

Moon Swan paused a long moment before answering.

"Oh, she'll find a way, I'm sure. She has *to find a way -- or else everyone in the entire Realm will be destroyed by the Hyradians. They make act easy-going in their demeanor, but when it comes to warfare, they take no prisoners!! I* can *make a suggestion, however."*

"And, uh, what's that?" I asked.

Then a slight smile crossed Moon Swan's face.

"They're very vainglorious. They want nothing more than total power and achievement of fame.

Use that 'characteristic' to your advantage."

That was easier said than done, as I was to soon find out…

CHAPTER TWELVE

For day after day we waited for the first sign of the Hyradian airship to arrive in our skies. The growing tension made us very unnerved. My Dad's strong resolve slowly melted away, leaving him a total nervous wreck.

Oddly enough on my part, I kept very calm about it all. I knew that I *had* to protect our entire Realm, nutty Wingy-Ding and all. In fact, I was rather looking forward to it. Of course, my Mom didn't still see it that way. That used to bother me, but not any more.

Even odder yet, Moon Swan actually became almost . . . *euphoric* about it all, as if she was getting some long-overdue justice that had been denied her for some long amount of time, although she didn't exactly say so out loud.

My Dad then recovered some of his British resolve and turned to me.

From the words of Mr. Steve Hackett:

As Skywatcher just told you readers earlier, I did indeed lose my nerve somewhat as we waited and waited for signs of trouble from those -- what were they again? -- Hyradians, that's it. It was eating us all alive. Even my wife was feeling the bite of fear—but she'd deny it all, as a matter of course. I knew the actual truth of it, sorry to admit.

But just at that moment, from out of the clear blue nowhere, Sunleaf turned to me, and then

embraced the very stuffings out of me. Then she did something else that I never dreamed she'd

do: she allowed her *real* emotions to flow outwards.

"Steve, I don't know about you, but I'm scared for my baby," she said.

"I know, Sunleaf. But she's a growing young woman, and a strong descendant of your race.

She'll pull it off all right," I replied soothingly.

That was all we were to say, for at that precise moment -- *there they were!!* The Hyradians

arrived and they were ready for everything . . . and in their eyes, may the Fates help those who

stand in the way of their total conquest and annihilation!!

It was all up to our daughter now.

This was her moment. And hers alone . . .

Here M. Ruther, Captain of the Royal Guardian Army tells his tale:

After we were summoned by his alleged "majesty" I rounded up my troops and stood watch at

our tower-posts, growing increasingly unnerved by the long pause that was sure to be exploited

by the enemy. But I tried not to let it personally faze me all that much. After all, it wouldn't be

the proper, if not English thing to do. The entire Realm was at risk.

(Of course, I'm telling you all this whilst the time was still opportune for us, as it were. And unknownst to us, young Skywatcher and her parents were yet within the confines of our castle, so I'm sure they'd seen it all firsthand.)

Then at that precise moment -- *the enemy had struck!!*

"Okay, lads, fall in, one at a time, defend this Realm, Noble Beings and all, with all the might and strength you've got . . . *and let no trace of the enemy remain about!* Fight to the last man!! And I mean, the very last man!!" shouted I to my men.

I was to soon find out that those words became eerily prophetic indeed.

For then, I saw that monolithic airship, just armed to the teeth.

This was truly not to be an ordinary fight, by any means…

From Skywatcher's diary:

I don't mind telling you, my eyes just *boggled* in fear upon first seeing that Hyradian airship in person. It turned out to be a lot more menacing that I first expected.

I turned around to look at King Wingy-Ding's castle, and distantly I saw Capt. Ruther's men

make ready to defend their home at all costs. I can bet they were as scared as I was, but of course

soldiers usually don't show too much fear. Or do they?

It was then that Moon Swan appeared to me once more.

"Your moment is here, Skywatcher. Are you ready?"

Inwardly I gulped down as much of my fear as possible.

"Okay . . . I'm ready," I said somewhat meekly.

She then placed her hands on my face.

"All right then, young one. Look up to the skies . . . and your true *courage will come to you*

when the timing is perfect." She sighed in pain, as the tears rolled down her face.

Then she drew me close to her, and hugged me tightly, weeping loudly…

CHAPTER THIRTEEN

From the Log of Robrack, commander of the Hyradian Army:

I can't even begin to tell you goody-goodies how we felt the moment the Foxtrot Time Works

entered our viewing scopes. It was getting everything you wanted for Christmas even though you

didn't actually deserve it.

That very moment, my dumpy head man Joe waltzed into my control room.

"Is everything set for our run?" I asked.

"Yeah, sure is. Anything else you want?" he replied blandly.

"Just make sure the boys do some maximum damage -- but *not* to our prize. Is that understood?"

"Sure thing, monster," he said flippantly.

"Uh, that's 'yes master,' Joe."

"Hey," he snorted, "I get paid to do your dirty work, not to massage your massive ego." Then he

left the control room, leaving me to seethe in anger.

I tell you right now, good, cheap henchmen are so hard to come by in these economic uncertainties…

From Skywatcher's diary:

A steely resolve, such as I never had before, now flowed throughout my mind. I felt more than ready.

I turned to my parents, my new resolve still in my being.

"Well, this is it," I said. "The prophecy is now coming true."

My Mom grabbed my arms and shook me till my brains rattled.

"Skywatcher, for the sake of the Fates, don't do this! *Please!*" she said to me, clearly frightened out of her wits.

In a show of defiance, I ignored her and turned to my Dad.

"Dad, you know why I'm doing this, right?" I asked him.

He didn't reply at first. That made me more than a little nervous.

"Well, love, logically I know, but that doesn't imply that I have to like it at all. Not by a long shot. And what if something tragic occurs? Has *that* thought entered into your brain? Well, has it?" I could really sense his growing fear of the inevitable, but I kept my cool about it. Like he would have, I think.

"To be frankly honest, Dad . . . uh, no. It hasn't."

Sadly he sighed again. He knew now that this *has* to be done -- for all our sakes. Mine, my parents, and everyone in the entire Realm depended on me.

And there was no way I was going to disappoint them . . .

CHAPTER FOURTEEN

"From life alone to life as one, think not now your journey's done. For though your ship be sturdy, no mercy has the sea..."

Peter Gabriel & Tony Banks, "Watcher of the Skies" from **Foxtrot**, 1972

From the words of Mr. Steve Hackett:

I can tell you right now that I *definitely* was not thrilled about the events that were soon to occur. The biggest downer of all, though, was doubtlessly my daughter's safety and welfare. I thought that if I were to start anew -- well, let's not dwell on that, shall we?

Anyway, there was nothing I could have done to prevent this. Plus, I know I should not utter a word of this but you can thank my wife, and her strange race of flying Amazon-minded broads for this.

Of course, I dare not say this to Sunleaf. At least, not to her face …

From Sunleaf's words:

Did you ever get that gnawing sense of a great loss coming your way? Well, that's exactly what happened to me at that moment when Skywatcher made her mind up to fulfill that sickening so-called "prophecy" that Moon Swan planted in my kid's brain. Naturally, I still wasn't thrilled by anything at this point. Yet that husband of mine was actually showing his true side instead of that English "reserve" he's so noted for. I had to admit, he really came through for me -- and our baby girl.

And that was a good thing, too, because she defintitely needed us now at this, the most crucial moment in her life.

I can only imagine what she was feeling by then.

From Skywatcher's diary:

I had already made up my mind to go through with Moon Swan's prophetic fulfillment. Now there was no more time to be having any second thoughts.

I closed my eyes, so as to clear my thoughts and bringing them into sharp focus. It was absolutely necessary to do this.

Then I re-opened my eyes.

I stretched my arms to the sky . . . and thus I was airborne.

Now it's all up to me -- and me alone.

Or so I thought at the time, anyway.

From the Log of Robrack, Commander of the Hyradian Army:

The moment our scan-scopes detected the Foxtrot Time Works, my excitement went up a staggering 400%. In spite of my somewhat gruff exterior, inside I was feeling euphorically giddy. How often do your plans come true in the way you actually conceive?

But I should have known that all good things don't last.

And just *why* am I telling you all of this, you ask?

Well, because our scan-scope operator turned and called out to me.

"Something on our scopes, Cap," he said out loud.

Speedily I raced up to him. Of course, that dumpy head man of mine just *had* to show up again, didn't he?

"What is it?" I asked.

"I don't know for certain. It's some kind of tiny blip."

"Well, what do you *think* it is?"

My so-called wise man sashayed his way to our scan-scope. What he told us sent us reeling in our senses.

"If I can venture a guess, I'd say it was -- "

"Well, what *is* it?!" I impatiently demanded.

He turned and gave me the most annoying grin in the history of human facial expressions.

"From what I can guess it's a flying girl. She's real cute, too."

"A flying *WHAT*?! What in the name of our realm have you been eating and drinking, as if I had to ask?"

"Just what I got done saying. A flying girl. And like I said, she's -- "

"Yeah. She's real cute, too. She could *also* make trouble. For you see, my alleged sage, she's probably from the sickeningly noble Startian race of bird-brained goody-goodies. And they don't like people like us. As if you had to be reminded."

"Well, there's only one thing left for me to do," said Joe with that flippancy intact.

"And what's that?" I asked him.

Before answering, he turned to the bridge's exit. And I did *not* like what he said afterwards.

"Sorry, 'boss,' but…I quit. 'Bye, y'all."

And he left. Just like that.

It was to me no matter. I didn't need his pea-brained advice anyway.

I had bigger things to achieve . . . and no flying kid would stop me!!

CHAPTER FIFTEEN

From Skywatcher's diary:

The moment I was airborne, I felt at home in the sky. It was *great!!*

But I knew that feeling wouldn't last too long, because at that very point I made contact with the airship that Moon Swan showed me in her vision. And let me tell you right now, folks, it was *scary!!*

Then again, I had no time for scaredy-cat-like fear. I was going to do my job -- and actually enjoy it as much as I can.

In a few seconds I landed on top of the airship as quietly as possible. Boy, were these Hyradians in for a heck of a rude surprise, I thought to myself . . .

I could hear the sounds of yelling and arguing in the control cabin right below where I was standing. It struck me as the funniest thing I'd ever heard.

"Listen, you, you go and find that flying brat *NOW!!!*" said a gruff, bossy voice.

I knew for a fact it belonged to their leader. In my mind, he acted like a cry-baby, but I heeded Moon Swan's warning about underestimating their intentions.

Swiftly I climbed down to the cabin and snuck my way inside. Boy oh boy, what a lot of gadgets it had. Just all nice and new, not to mention dangerous as well. It was empty at the time, though I sensed it wouldn't stay that way for long…

Then a high, whiny voice shouted out.

"Hey, you!! You're not allowed in here!!"

I turned around, and I saw a tall guy with long black hair, brown eyes, and a uniform of some kind or other.

It was the pilot. A real shame, too, cause I thought he was rather cute…for a bad guy, anyway.

I gave him my best cute girliest smile.

"Who says I need permission anyway? You? I don't think so!"

"Why, you, I'll -- wait a minute! You're that flying kid, ain't you?"

"My name's Skywatcher, you meathead! Learn how to use it!"

Then the pilot grabbed me by my arm. I wanted to bite his ear!

"Come here, you brat! We're going to see someone," he hissed.

Soon he led me away…

Here M. Ruther, Captain of the Royal Guardian Army, tells more of his tale:

After we saw Skywatcher land on the airship, our hearts grew black with worry. Inwardly I realized that this was no mission for such a young kid to undertake on her own. I can just imagine the traumatic ordeal her parents were dealing with. In fact, I *know* what it's like, believe me on that.

Within seconds our eyes gazed toward the near entrance of our castle. Here were Mr. and Mrs. Hackett entering back inside and climb their way to the tower-posts. The look of fear on their faces was painfully clear.

Mr. Hackett was the first to approach me.

"Did you see any further trace of Skywatcher?" asked he, worriedly.

"No, not quite yet, Mr. Hackett, but I'm hopeful that she's safe." He sensed that I was not convincing in that assurance. But, of course, this was no time to disappoint the Hacketts. That wouldn't be the English thing to do now, would it?

From that moment onwards, my inner resolve grew stronger…

From Sunleaf's words:

That dreadful feeling in my stomach intensified with each passing moment. What's happening to my baby? Why her?

Steve did his trying best to assure me.

"Remember what I said, Sunleaf. Our daughter is a strong young lady. She'll handle it all right," he said. Naturally I didn't believe it. I was too sick with worry and fear. I mean, that's my child up there.

Just wait until I get my hands on Moon Swan.

She's gonna *pay!!*

CHAPTER SIXTEEN

From Skywatcher's diary:

That snot-faced pilot dragged me to a door and knocked as loud as it could go. Strangely enough, I wasn't at all scared.

"What is it *now*?!!" It was the boss's voice.

"Cap, I got a present for you," said the pilot.

Instantly the door opened up, and out stepped a tall guy, decked out like a drum major. Either that or a wannabe Civil War general. He had short brown hair, hazelish eyes, and sideburns going past his ears. He also was not too happy to see me.

"So you're the flying brat due to make trouble," he said to me.

I gave him a nasty look.

"I just got done telling your pilot, and now I'll tell you. My name's Skywatcher. Get it into your cave-sized empty skulls."

He -- the boss, that is -- grew really mad now.

"Listen here, you splumpering little brat!! You don't *ever* talk to a grown-up like that!" he boomed.

"Why not? I just did that to you, didn't I?"

In a few seconds he cooled down.

"Let's get something straight now. First of all, I think you're a rude little kid and second, where do you get off attacking my ship?"

Then I grew serious.

"It's simple. You're going to attack and destroy the Foxtrot Time Works. *That's* something I won't allow you to do, you space-age pansy!"

"And just why not?" he retorted.

I eyed him in the sternest way imaginable.

"The reasons are that first, it would destroy the entire Universe of the Time Beyond Time and second--"

"Yes?"

I paused a moment before answering.

"Well, second is that -- *my Dad works there!!* Now, you satisfied, fathead?! Huh?!" I thought I showed him. I was wrong.

"Hey, you," he said, turning to the pilot, "take Little Miss Smart-Mouth here and throw her in the brig, or overboard, I really don't care which. Just get rid of her!"

This guy made a big mistake . . .

From the Logs of Robrack, Hyradian Army Commander:

After my distasteful meeting with that flying brat, I returned to the control cabin and resumed my focusing on the Foxtrot Time Works.

I can only hope that *this* time there would be no more trouble…

CHAPTER SEVENTEEN

Now Tony, doorman/pianist to 'King' Weigndin, relates his story:

Well, all I can tell you is that events had transpired so fast it's impossible to know where to start. I mean, I'm a pianist, not a story writer by any means. But out of good manners, I'll do the best that I can under some truly weird circumstances.

After the party had (fortunately for myself, I can say) ended somewhat abruptly, I began to remember my own family, having just met Skywatcher and her family. I had a daughter of my own, and only the Fates know what I'd do if anything harmful happened to her. I can just, rightly so, imagine what the Hacketts were enduring at this stage.

However, getting back to my part in the story I went up to his royal "majesty" to try to calm him down after the rather unexpected panic bout he'd just experienced upon finally realizing the peril about to unfold around us.

(Of course, I continually had to shout into his malfunctioning ears just to make myself understood.)

"Sire," I said rather loudly, "our men will take care of the event. Try to relax, if you please."

He gave me his trademark peculiar look.

"What's that? Sneeze? I don't have to sneeze."

Inwardly I groaned. How much more of this can I take?

"Sire . . . " I sighed, then shouted, "GET YOUR EARS MENDED, HUH?!?" Then I stormed out of his sloppily-decorated throne-room and made my way to the tower-posts, where Capt. Ruther and his men were standing by, preparing to fight off the attack force now making its path toward us. In an instant, I turned my eyes skyward and there, right above me I saw the airship, fully armed. A rather majestic sight, I thought, in a strange manner.

I only hoped that girl Skywatcher knew what she's in for…

From Skywatcher's diary:

I was led into the brig, and then thrown in rather roughly. The door slammed, and I was trapped. But I wasn't at all frightened.

And why wasn't I frightened, you ask?

Well…I'll let you in on a little secret. You see, I know someone very special. He said if I ever needed him, just use some special chant or other and he'll show up, no questions asked. But for now, I didn't think to do so. It wasn't necessary.

And so, with nothing much else to do, I looked around the brig, coming to a viewing window. I could see King Wingy-Ding's castle below me, with Captain Ruther's troops ready to attack the airship.

Then from out of nowhere, a friendly voice called out.

"So you're the one named Skywatcher, I see."

I glanced at a short, dumpy-looking guy with short grey hair, blue eyes, and an easy-going smile on his face. I smiled back, trying to be friendly.

"Hi. What's your name?" I asked.

"Joe. My name's Joe. You're not going to believe this, but I know the guy who's running this invasion."

"Yeah, we met. That's why I'm in here now."

"Well, all I can say, for now, is that, frankly, he deserved it. And he *knows* it, too." Then his smile disappeared.

"How did you come to be in here?" I asked Joe.

"Well…I was about to depart the ship, having suddenly announced my resignation as Robrack's alleged 'advisor.' He only wanted me to kiss up to him and his universe-sized ego. I don't have to tell you that I didn't get very far, and that's due to the fact that his pouty-pussed pilot grabbed me and threw me into the brig. *And* I found myself stuck with -- *him*," he responded, pointing at last to a long-brown-haired guy, in white face paint and black jumpsuit. He pranced around like a drunken scarecrow. It was almost funny…if I didn't feel sorry for him. He looked rather depressed.

"Lam-dee-dum-dee-dandy day . . ." he said, over and over.

I turned back to Joe.

"What happened to him?"

Joe paused sadly before answering.

"You can thank Robrack for this. That's why he has to be stopped." He grew angry then. Oh, how he hated Robrack.

I smiled as wide as I could.

"Oh, don't worry about that, Joe. I'll stop him."

I just had to figure out how…

CHAPTER EIGHTEEN

From the logs of Robrack, Commander of the Hyradian Army:

The Foxtrot Time Works was within my sight, courtesy of my scan-scope and no thanks to that stupid, idiotic pilot of mine. Swiftly I made my way to the main observation window, and lo and behold, *there it was!!* A vast array of complex technology, housed in a spacious Art Deco-style layout.

I had to admit, it was really impressive . . . despite the fact that my resident arch-foe, namely that flying little brat, said her old man worked there. Of course, I didn't care in the slightest bit.

And it was all *mine for the taking!!!*

I quickly shouted out to my men.

"All right, men, get the lead out. Activate the octo-lasers and start wiping whatever you see out of existence . . . except the Foxtrot Time Works. *That's* the main prize. Now…" I stated, "go to work, boys!!"

Let the Chaos begin!!!

Here M. Ruther, Captain of the Royal Guardian Army, relates more of his tale:

There was the briefest of pauses before one of my troops shouted.

"Sir!! Three degrees west bogey!! It's *him,* sir!!"

I turned about and found myself gazing on the enemy airship, firing his weapon downward on the land, laying siege and waste to all that made contact.

My resolve grew more steely and staunch than ever.

"Fire at will!!" I shouted.

I have to say right now, my men showed the greatest dedication and aplomb in their assigned tasks. Swiftly they fired shot after shot, aiming directly at the ship. But much to our collective chagrin, the retalitory shots fired had no effect. The blaggards had somehow generated a massive force-field screen 'round the ship.

I started having a feeling I didn't like.

"Sir, our shots aren't stopping it," said my lead-man.

Privately I felt this was a battle we couldn't win.

But of course, defeat isn't the English way to go.

I silently prayed to the Fates that young Skywatcher's courage holds up. We're counting on her, and she on us.

Gritting my teeth tightly, I turned back to my troops.

They had gotten the message. They kept firing…and firing.

And so it went . . .

From Skywatcher's diary:

The rumbling of battle reached our ears quickly. Joe and I were trying to work out our escape plan. Idea after idea was bounced around until a silly thought entered my mind, and it had something to do with our prancing scarecrow with the white face-paint and long brown hair.

"Hey!! Hey!!" I yelled.

Swiftly someone raced down. It was that cute-looking yet snotty pilot; he didn't look too happy to see me again.

"Yeah, what do you want, kid?!" he hissed.

"My friend here," I said, indicating the dancing scarecrow, "has to go to the bathroom -- and I mean *now*."

He gave me a sort of "I don't believe you" look on his face.

"A likely story," he actually said.

Then Joe interceded.

"It's true, Randolph. You've gotta get him to the restroom, or else it's -- " he said, holding his nostrils together.

Randolph, the pilot, rolled up his eyes in disgust.

"Oh, all right. Just a minute," he stated wearily.

Man, did he make a big mistake 'cause you see, the second Randolph opened up the brig's door immediately I kept my promise to myself and bit his ear. Not off, but enough to make him yowl like one of those old-time DJs on your 1970s radio music programs. Then we -- Joe and I, that is -- ran him down.

Halfway into our escape run, we'd forgotten something -- or some *one*.

"Hey, where's our dancing scarecrow friend?" I asked Joe.

Without missing a beat, Joe returned to the brig and grabbed our friend. Then, having caught up to where I stood we resumed our run.

Now I can resume my quest . . . and keep my promise to Moon Swan, wherever she may be at this time.

CHAPTER NINETEEN

From the words of Mr. Steve Hackett:

My wife's gnawing paranoid worry started to concern me at a rather furious rate. All this long amount of time I told myself and Sunleaf that our daughter was going to pull through this all right.

That was before I saw the Hyradian airship fire its weapons on our land, destroying house, supermarket, library, *et al.* The only thing *not* being hit was the Foxtrot Time Works. I initially couldn't figure out why.

Then, somewhat slowly, the horrifying truth dawned on me.

That was no doubt what the Hyradians want. It's been said (though not by myself) that whoever controls the Foxtrot Time Works has total domination of the entire Realm of the Time Beyond Time. These -- *monsters* want to destroy our whole Realm, just for power and control.

It was the most sickening realization I'd ever had.

Now my own worry for my daughter's safety grew obsessively all-consuming, thus enabling me to fully understand my wife's concern. And there wasn't thing one I could do about it.

Or was there?

Here Tony, doorman/pianist for King Wingy-Ding, tells more of his tale:

Having just made my way to the tower-posts, as I related to you earlier, I glanced at Captain Ruther and his troops fire shot after shot from their powerful laser-staffs at the enemy airship, yet they'd absolutely no bearing on it at all.

All at once, a nauseating sense ovewhelmed me. It wasn't a physical nausea, but rather a tad on the psychological side. Naturally, I didn't enjoy having such a sense in me.

But it wasn't for myself that I grew emotionally ill.

No, it was for the Hacketts' young daughter, trying her truest best to stop these hideous-minded invaders from destroying the entire Realm.

Oh, Skywatcher, don't let us down now . . .

From Sunleaf's words:

Let me say to you right now that I became increasingly agitated and frustrated at everything that went on . . . not to mention scared to death. I mean, that's my *baby* up there, suffering a Fates-know-what kind of trouble. And all this you can thank Moon Swan for. I tell you now, if I wasn't distantly related to her, I'd sue her sorry behind.

But a lawsuit isn't going to keep my child safe. That much I know.

At least I had Steve with me, trying to comfort me even though he could use some of that

himself. I can see that on his face.

That…and a few tears rolling down…

CHAPTER TWENTY

From Skywatcher's diary:

The three of us jogged our way into the control room. There we saw Robrack look down on all the trouble he's causing. And he was smiling! Boy, I couldn't wait to get him, but as to how I would do it well, I didn't have a clue. Not yet, anyway.

Unless . . . yeah. Of course!

Joe saw in my eyes what I was thinking. And he didn't like it.

"Skywatcher, what are you -- ?" he began. I didn't wait around to hear him finish his thought. I grabbed our prancing scarecrow, and presently snuck my way inside the room. Just right smack behind ol' Sour-Puss the Crabby Captain himself. Instantly the scarecrow hippie pranced around.

"Lam-dee-dum-dee-dandy day," he said, again and again.

Slowly Robrack turned and just couldn't believe his senses. He was calm at first, then grew really angry. And he said so, in no uncertain terms whatsoever.

"Who the blazes let *this* thing out of the brig?!" he spluttered.

From out of the blue I replied out to him.

"Who wants to know?"

He whirled around, and he did *not* grow any happier.

"Why, you little snot, I'm going to -- " he snarled as he tried to grab me. I ducked underneath him, and ran out of the control room, leaving Joe and the prancing hippie behind for only a moment. Then they caught up to where I was. The hippie was still doing his nutty routine, getting on Joe's last nerve.

"Oh, why don't you shut up?!" he yelled. Balling up his fist, he bopped the hippie on the head.

And then a strange thing occurred …

The prancing hippie had regained his senses!!

"What happened? Why did you hit me on the head?!"

Joe turned to the hippie.

"Well, you see, your act was staring to get just a little old, and we -- well, *I* decided it was time to pull the plug."

"Well … thanks," said the hippie. Then he turned to me. "What's your name, kid? Not to be rude or some such, but -- "

"It's Skywatcher Hackett. What's your name?" I queried.

"It's Peter," he said.

"Peter what?"

Peter grew mad slightly, sighing heavily.

"It's Peter Piper picked a peck of pickled peppers. *Now what do you THINK it is?!!"* he yelled. And let me tell you, I don't like being yelled at.

I didn't say anything after that. Then Joe intervened.

"First of all, she's a kid, and a good one at that. Second, she wasn't being rude or crass, just curious. I hope you see your way to realize that."

"Well . . . all right. No harm done."

I turned back to Joe.

"What made him the way he was?" I asked.

"It's a long story, as I said, but suffice it to say you can thank Robrack for making him the way he was. But now he's okay, thanks to you, young lady."

I couldn't help but smile at that one.

But it would be the last smile for a long time.

I had to stop Robrack. Now.

CHAPTER TWENTY-ONE

From Sunleaf's words:

My nerves grew more and more raw with each passing moment. I hated this feeling of just standing by, doing nothing while my child is up there on this now-life threatening mission given to her.

Swiftly my fear and worry gave way to a new resolve.

I turned my gaze to that monstrous airship, knowing that my baby was fighting for her life against these marauders.

I planned a course of action fueled by my maternal instinct.

It didn't take me long to execute it.

Silently I closed my eyes, a faint smile radiating from my face even as my slightly-aged wings unfurled. Then I outstretched my arms to the starry nighttime skies.

Steve sternly looked at me, not liking what he saw.

"Sunleaf, don't do anything rash. Just don't."

Against my matrimonial duties I ignored him. Slowly I lifted off the ground in a near-ecstatic moment.

Then . . . I was airborne. *One with the sky,* I thought to myself.

The last thing I heard was Steve calling out to me.

"SUNLEAF!! SUNLEAF!!!"

No, Steve. As much as I love you, not this time . . .

From the words of Mr. Steve Hackett:

From the moment I saw Sunleaf take to the skies in the way she did, I knew then that I *had* to do my part in helping my only daughter fulfill that mission Moon Swan gave to Skywatcher. I mean, I *am* her father, am I not?

The only quandary was: *how?*

I just didn't have the answer. As yet, anyway…

M. Ruther, Captain of the Royal Guardian Army, relates more of his tale:

The battle had raged for what seemed like hours without end, and not one gain of ground on either end. But of course, my lads wouldn't dare dream of surrender. These were highly trained soldiers, dedicated to the cause of right.

It was at that exact moment that I caught sight of a flying object, faint in the distance. Grabbing my spectra-field binoculars I was able to get a sharper look. And my jaw totally dropped!

Swiftly I shouted out to my lads.

"Hold fire, men! There's a civilian up there."

Mr. Hackett walked up beside me. I turned to him.

"Mr. Hackett, do you know that's your missus up there?"

He nodded wearily, already painfully aware of the fact.

"Yes," was all he stated. He looked forlorn at that state.

Out of sympathetic kindness, I placed my hand on his shoulder.

"I'm sure she'll be all right. Quite a special missus you have," I said to him reassuringly.

"That much I know already. I just hope she returns to hear that."

Returning my sight to the enemy I scanned the sky and, fortunately, found no trace of Sunleaf.

Surmising that she had made her way to that airship, I had my lads resume firing … for all the little good it would do by then.

Inwardly I felt it was a losing battle. Admitting *that*, I determined, is definitely not the English way to victory now, is it?

From Skywatcher's diary:

I re-entered Robrack's control room, looking around at all the equipment and machines that even now caused so much havoc, as Moon Swan predicted. There were levers, dials, touch-screens, keyboards, monitors, and diodes.

I had to admit, it was fascinating … in a very wicked sense. I became lost in all that wonder when that harsh familiar voice shouted out from behind where I stood.

"SO!! I have you at long last, you little snit!!" It was Robrack.

I turned around and sneered at him.

"Big deal. Now what are going to do with me? Huh?"

Then from out of the hallway Randolph waltzed in, getting an angry, snarling look from his boss.

"Where the blazes were *YOU* at?!!?"

"Well . . . " said Randolph, "I was in the med-room."

"WHAT?!!? Why, as if I had to ask?"

"You see, I got bit on my ear. And she's the one who bit me. The young snot," Randolph replied, pointing at me.

Robrack returned his gaze to me.

"You have no idea how much you're going to suffer for all the trouble you've caused up to now. And there isn't anyone in this Universe, or any other, that can save you now." Looking at Randolph, Robrack yelled, "You!! Grab that kid!!"

Out of nowhere Joe and Peter zipped in between us.

"Don't do this, Robrack." That's what Joe said.

Robrack smiled in a very greasily smug manner.

"Well, well, well. My hare-brained ex-advisor and my pet dancing scarecrow have taken up for the kid. Well, I hope you're happy with that choice because now you'll join her in her demise. Any last words of courage?"

"Yeah, just this," retorted Joe. "I regret that I didn't shave off your left sideburn and shove it up your right nostril. Now *that* would be a sight to see."

Furious, Robrack ordered Randolph to carry out the plan for our end. Swiftly Randolph snatched some rope, and tied Joe's and Peter's arms together. Then he made his way to me. He was now armed with a small laser-knife. Sneering, he was about to do what I would rather not say. Then all at once my courage, for the first time, faltered …

And then -- *I made my special move.*

"Epoch, laidan turloghar dubh!!" I yelled.

Randolph paused in his movement. *That* was his mistake.

You see, there appeared a thin jet-black trail of smoke landing right behind him. Then it grew and morphed into the shape of a man. This man was now becoming more distinct. He was tall, thin, with dark-brown hair and Celtic blue eyes. Dressed all in black he was, and armed with a ruby sword. *And*...he never smiled. It was, of course, our own legendary Swordsman of Time named Epoch.

Randolph was beside himself in confusion...but for only a brief moment. Then he lunged out at Epoch, but Epoch casually side-stepped aside and tripped Randolph.

He then drew out his sword, and chanted:

"Heartless pilot, by north or south, say no further and close your mouth!"

Instantly a cloth handkerchief formed around Randolph's mouth. He tried to scream for help yet all he said was, "Mmmph!! Flmmphmph mmph flmmphmph!!" (I won't translate *that* for you. Sorry.)

I turned to Epoch. He got the message, smiled slightly, and returned to his own Realm. (And now you know the secret that I promised to tell you earlier.)

Unknown to us, all this didn't go unnoticed by Robrack.

"I don't know what you did, but you won't get a chance to repeat that little stunt!" snarled

Robrack. Then he drew out his own sword, as well as his laser-pistol.

Then all looked bleak for me…

CHAPTER TWENTY-TWO

From Sunleaf's words:

Somewhere on that ship my child had to be nearby. A mother's instinct is seldom wrong on these

things, and I *knew* that it had to come through for me on this. I mean, this is my *baby* I'm talking

about here.

For a few seconds I fluttered around the airship, searching for any means of access into it. Then

immediately, I found it!

Pushing all other thoughts aside, I landed on the gangway of the ship's port. There my eyes

widened in fear!!

It was then I saw Skywatcher, with two friends of hers, about to be taken by some dandy pirate.

But I knew he really *wasn't* some dandy…but a scourge and festering cancer on our entire

Realm.

Then I witnessed that nasty scum actually -- *oh Fates, NO!!*

That's when I really lost it.

Speedily I flew in, and finally came face-to-whatever he had on his puss. He didn't look to happy to see what he saw next.

"Don't you touch my BABY!!!" I screeched, even as I decked him.

Skywatcher turned to see me.

"Mom!!" she squealed in delight, hugging me.

The scuzzball recovered his wits. He eyed us questioningly.

"What is it with you winged women anyway??!" he queried.

Skywatcher turned to him, grinning that grin she's always had.

"Oh, this is my mom," she said, "and we 'winged women' always watch out for each other."

Then she turned back to me. "Oh, Mom, this is Robrack, the enemy," she stated. I wasn't pleased to meet him at all. Not after what he tried to do.

Robrack snarled at us. I did *not* like what he had in mind . . .

From the words of Mr. Steve Hackett:

The sense of hopelessness grew increasingly prevalent in my psyche as events continued to unfold. I saw Captain Ruther try his utmost best to keep the Hyradian airship at bay, though we all knew it was a losing cause. And I was rather irritated at Sunleaf for pulling off that rash stunt of hers. She'd put herself in grave danger…and I do mean *grave*.

I then got a sense of eerieness about me. Whirling around I was met with that strange yet familiar glowing I encountered much, much earlier. In a flash of time I realized who it was. The voice confirmed this for my own peace of mind, albeit temporarily.

"Hello, Stephen. We meet again." It was Moon Swan.

I slowly turned around. It was then she got a good look of the glum expression on my face, which was also mixed with anger.

"Well, I hope you're happy with yourself. Not only is my young daughter's life in jeopardy thanks to you, but now my wife has just gone up to the airship to help Skywatcher," I stated flatly if not somewhat tersely.

Moon Swan gazed at me in a most peculiar manner.

"No, Stephen, I am most emphatically not *happy by these events as they're transpiring. But* you *may be able to play a key part in its outcome, whatever it may be."* Then, oddly enough, she actually grinned at me, though I didn't know why . . . yet.

Then she drew herself close to me.

"Hold out your hands, Stephen. I wish to give you the one thing you'll need in aiding your family in this arduous task that I so carelessly brung onto you."

Presently I did so, and soon I was surrounded by a very intense force of light that seemed to emanate directly from Moon Swan herself. I don't mind telling you good readers now that it blinded me immensely.

When I later regained my sight, I was confronted by an even stranger sight. In my arms was -- my old Gibson Les Paul electric guitar!! I hadn't played it since my halcyon university band days, just before I met and married Sunleaf.

Grateful as I was, I couldn't help but remain curious.

"Uh, Moon Swan, what's with this old guitar of mine?!"

Moon Swan just about laughed her head off at that.

"You see, Stephen, this *is your weapon of choice. The reason is because I just realized the Hyradians don't like rock music, and I figured since you mentioned you wanted to aid your young daughter and rescue your wife, well --* " I stopped her right there.

"Say no more."

It was time for me to be a true dad...

CHAPTER TWENTY-THREE

Here Tony, King Wingy-Ding's doorman/pianist, tells more of his tale:

I was standing next to Mr. Hackett when his rather unusual "gift" was handed to him by a tall, long-haired beauty in plain suede garb, with what appeared to be wings growing from out her shoulders. I must say, she was even quite attractive; sort of like a young Ali MacGraw or Sarah Douglas-type. Maybe even a young, brunette Helen Mirren-type.

I wanted to introduce myself to her, but of course I didn't at first. Then she turned round to me and smiled quite broadly.

"Hello, my name's Tony," I said.

"Hello, Tony. I am Moon Swan. I'm Skywatcher's maternal ancestor, and I'm also responsible for all this havoc we're all in right now."

Maternal ancestor, she said. Oh wow.

Swiftly my eyes returned to the battle at hand … just as Moon Swan and Mr. Hackett both *vanished into thin air*!!

From Sunleaf's words:

I was more than ready to pound Robrack's ugly face some more, in spite of the fact that he was armed with a laser-pistol. As if *that* would stop me, I thought to myself in grim delight. Again he smiled that nauseatingly smug grin.

Then he charged his gun.

He pulled the trigger, then…a faint crunching rhythm was felt throughout the airship. Robrack halted, trying to look around. As did we, of course.

To my own chagrin, I immediately knew what that was. I turned around and there behind us, my husband, with not only Moon Swan with him, but also -- *his old electric guitar!!*

I stood there, laughing at such a sight.

Unfortunately, Robrack wasn't so amused. Not by a long shot.

"*NOW* what's going on here?!" he spluttered.

Presently Moon Swan made herself be known.

"*Hello, all,*" was all she said for now. Then my daughter ran to Steve, hugging the living stuffings out of him as usual.

"Daddy!!!" she squealed loudly.

Robrack was now just beside himself.

"You've got to be *kidding* me, right?!"

Happily we ignored him.

Big mistake on our part . . .

CHAPTER TWENTY-FOUR

M. Ruther, Captain of the Royal Guardian Army, relates more of his story:

For hours on end our war dragged. My men, staunch as they are, had reached the breaking point and were about to call it a loss. Of course, as I've stated many a time throughout, "surrender" is not the English way to go. My men knew it, but also realized that victory was not at all that easy to achieve.

Presently one of my troops turned 'round to me.

"Sir, request to speak freely," he said.

"Granted."

He paused before speaking, as if he needed to weigh his words.

"Sir, I just don't see any way out other than withdrawing."

Sympathetically I placed my hand on his shoulder.

"I know, lad, but we must carry on."

"Sir, I understand, but why *are* we fighting?"

Now it was my turn to pause in reflection. I nodded firmly.

"For Skywatcher, lad. This is all for young Skywatcher."

He, too, nodded firmly. Then he carried on his fight … as did I.

From Skywatcher's diary:

I can't begin to tell you my feeling of joy when my Mom and Dad arrived with Moon Swan and weirdly enough, my Dad had his old guitar with him. *That* was a curious sight, let me tell you.

Then ol' sour-puss Robrack, still mad as ever, made himself be heard, whether we wanted it or not.

"Ahem. Sorry to cut this little family reunion short, but now it's time for me to destroy all of you. Even you, Joe … not that I actually liked you in the first place anyway," he snarled, drawing and charging his laser-pistol.

Smiling thinly and armed with his guitar, my Dad waltzed up to Robrack. He was eye-to-eye, then soon after that my Dad tuned the guitar.

Robrack's eyeballs widened in angry confusion, as my Dad gave a feel to the strings. It then registered on the Hyradian's psyche.

Then afterwards … my Dad started to play an old solo he'd created while still in his college prog-rock band. It was the perfect distraction needed.

Instantly Robrack plugged his ears with his fingers, and amidst the hysteria Moon Swan grabbed Joe and Peter, teleporting them to safety.

While my Dad still played more of his solo, Mom glanced around the control-room, and caught a glimpse of a rather out-of-place bucket of soapy water. How odd…and yet not really *that* strange, I thought.

(In a silly manner, it reminded me of Randolph, whom we'd left behind earlier, still muffling out his naughty words.)

Then, Robrack fired his pistol airward, stopping my Dad's solo.

"That does it, you little snot!!" he yelled. *That* earned him something he thought he'd never expected. For you see, the minute he said that, my Dad rammed his guitar into Robrack's stomach. You don't want to anger my Dad.

"What did you call her?" asked Dad, in an icy manner.

Robrack wasted no time in answering.

"What?!! Your little rock show make you deaf?!!?"

My Dad pummeled him again.

I thought it'd never end. How wrong, yet how -- *right* as well...

Then, unexpectedly, my Mom turned to me, bringing to mind the soapy water bucket. A broad grin radiated from her lovely face.

Smiling back, I nodded.

I got the message …

CHAPTER TWENTY-FIVE

Here Tony, King Wingy-Ding's pianist/doorman, tells more of his story:

I was still in a state of shock after seeing Moon Swan and Mr. Hackett vanish into thin air in the way they did, but that's par for the course. Hurriedly I descended back into reality, addressing Captain Ruther.

"How goes the battle?" I asked.

(It was then that, unbeknownst to me, King Wingy-Ding sashayed his way to our position.)

Captain Ruther sighed out heavily, as if in fear of answering.

"Well … it's going on a trifle bit long," he replied.

Then … *oh no!!*

"What?? A hit song?! I'll die silly if *this* becomes a hit song."

Our hard-of-hearing "leader" struck again, but for once he focused on the scene at hand. In a strange way he was courageous, I suppose…though that didn't mean I thought he was a good overall leader. But time always tells, I suppose.

Still, my heart ever goes out to you, Skywatcher. Always.

From Sunleaf's words:

Let me be the first to say to you that I got a doubly weird sense in my gut. I knew that my baby was safe but I also felt that a great change was going to happen … that is, if we get out of this first.

I know, I know…back to the adventure.

Skywatcher received my signal even as Steve ended both his concert and his sudden anger spell. I was in love with Steve all over again…and it was great! What a strong man he'd become in my eyes, and what a special child Skywatcher is for me…

This was her moment to shine.

From Skywatcher's diary:

The moment I picked up the water bucket, a new feeling had overcome me. I couldn't describe it at first, but I knew that my life was due to change quite soon. It's as if … I would no longer be the kid I was at the beginning.

Then, I made my move … and it felt like all time stopped.

I threw the water onto the control panel.

Robrack, of course, wasn't thrilled.

"Do you know what soapy water does to Hyradian electronics, young woman?" he queried in a sarcastically calm voice.

"No, but you'll tell me anyway," I retorted in the usual way.

Then Robrack exploded in rage.

"It eats through, you little witch!! You've wrecked everything for me!! Now you'll REALLY *pay!!! I'll sue you for every pinko cent you've got!!!"* Even as he announced his lawsuit, the entire room was showered with sparks from the exploding controls.

We were then forced to flee for our lives …

M.Ruther, Captain of the Royal Guardian Army, relates more of his tale:

A jubilant cheer erupted from my men as the first explosion from the airship made its visual way to their eyes. It indeed was a cause to cheer, though we realized the battle was not yet over.

Scanning into my spectra-field binoculars, I took note that the force-field was thus deactivated. *That* gave us new hope.

"Hit it with all, lads!!" I shouted to my troops. Swiftly, and with the typically English aplomb they showed, my men joyously responded, striking hit after hit! Inwardly, though, I worried about the Hacketts.

I hoped to the Fates that they'd made it out alive…

From the log of Robrack, commander of the Hyradian Army:

My control-panel exploded all around my ship, wreaking havoc on everything…including my dreams of conquest and dominion over this entire cursed Realm. That little brat and her nauseating entourage would suffer *immensely* for this, one way or another!!

Suddenly, my hapless "pilot" made his way to what was left of my airship…and I just wasn't in the mood to even look at him now! But, naturally I turned to him.

"Where the blazes -- *what happened to YOU?!*" I yelled.

"Mmmpfhlph, mmf fmmf Mmmphm!" he "said".

"WHAT?!!!?"

It was the last thing I would say to Randolph…because at that moment we turned and got a gaze at yet another of those winged women. And *this* one eyed us with all the rage she could muster.

"Robrack of the Hyradians, hear me now. As decreed by the Fates of Time I, Moon Swan of the Startian race, hereby place you under my people's guard." She didn't smile, even though I thought it was the funniest thing I'd ever heard … at the time anyway.

"Uh, and that means what?" I asked.

She walked up to us, smiling oh so slightly.

"That means, you jackass, you're under arrest. And so is Mr. Mumbles over here." Then she spread her arms out, and soon all went black. Or white, in this case...

M. Ruther, Captain of the Royal Guardian Army, concludes his tale:
I began to grow increasingly afright out of concern for the Hacketts even as the explosions from the enemy airship continued. It was as if all hope had gone.

Then, in the midst of my worry, one of my lads turned 'round to me, showing a rather agitated look from his young face.

"Sir!! Twelve degrees south bogey!"

I raced to his position, drawing my spectra-field binoculars to my eyes…and was joyously greeted by a quiet reassuring sight.

The Hacketts and friends were safe on land!!

Newly inspired, I stood taut and staunch.

"Right, lads . . . *hit it with it all!!!*" shouted I.

Let our victory be confirmed, and our Realm be safe.

Thank you, Skywatcher. Always.

From the words of Mr. Steve Hackett:

We found ourselves on land, intact, just mere momentsbefore the Hyradian airship was destroyed, no doubt thanks to the combined efforts of Captain Ruther's troops . . . and of course, our young special gift Skywatcher.

Speaking of whom, we looked around, after the dust had cleared, and Skywatcher was nowhere to be seen. This worried us, and rightly so.

"Sunleaf, where's Skywatcher?" I asked Sunleaf.

She turned to me and shook her head slowly. That meant that something happened to her, in spite of our total victory.

Immediately I felt a sense of despair gnawing at me.

From out of the blue, or black, that familiar yet eerie glow bathed Sunleaf and I. It was Moon Swan...and she brought forth a quite unexpected surprise.

"Hello, Stephen. You needn't worry about Skywatcher. She's quite safe, and wishes to speak to you."

Then a tall, young red-haired woman emerged from Moon Swan's aura. Was this---*our daughter?!*

"Hello, Father. Hello, Mother. It's me, Skywatcher."

I didn't like what was to come next . . .

From Sunleaf's words:

My jaw dropped when Skywatcher came up to us. I mean, she was so -- *different.* This was no longer the brash girl who dragged all of us into this epic adventure. This was a mature woman; stronger, wiser … and more noble.

"What -- what's *happened* to you?"

She wasted no time in answering…for what was the last time she would spend on our world.

"This is my new form now, Mother. I just wanted to say goodbye. I am to fulfill the new destiny that's ahead of me. Moon Swan told me of this just now, and well, I want all of you, even King Wingy-Ding and his friends, to know that I love you all so very much…and also I wish to thank Captain Ruther and Company for their staunch support."

(While all this was being said, Tony, Capt. Ruther and his troops, and especially that nutty Wingy-Ding made their way to us.)

Steve and I raced up to her, and we then embraced our baby for the last time. The tears really rolled down all our faces.

Tony, with King Wingy-Ding in tow, went to Skywatcher and placed his hand on her winged shoulder.

"Go now, our brave heroine. And may your courage and strength and love for us all last long."

He, too, shed many a tear.

Naturally, ol' King Wingy-Ding spoke out.

"Huh?? A fast song?? Okay, right, *hit it!!*"

And he was at it again.

This time, we all welcomed it even as Skywatcher took to the skies of the Time Beyond Time, never to return…

"Come ancient children, hear what I say. This is my parting council for you on your way."

Peter Gabriel & Tony Banks, "Watcher of the Skies" from **Foxtrot**, 1972

THE END

(for now, anyway)

GLOSSARY

NOTE: Many terms were used in the duration of our tale, and doubtless those terms may confuse the reader. Hence this guide to further your understanding.

ONE SIGN: in Startian religions, the forbidden Prophecy that signifies an accumulation of events so cataclysmic, it became Startian law to not divulge the Prophecy. Moon Swan defies this directive, setting off the adventures of Skywatcher and her loved ones.

OCTO-LASER: an eight-lensed laser, on an axle mechanism, similar to the late-19th century Gatling Machine Gun. The octo-laser fires a concentrated amount of radiating energy capable of atomizing all that enter its path.

STARTIAN: a race of winged women hailing from the planet Startia. The planet orbits the Castion sun at a rate comparable to that of our own Earth. More than half of the Startian women are of either American Indian or Hispanic-Irish descent, as in the cases of Moon Swan and Sunleaf, though there are those of Germanic or Celtic descent as well.

SPECTRA-FIELD BINOCULARS: a specially combined mix of high-field binoculars and television camera able to pick up all known spectrum variances, such as infra-red, ultraviolet, body heat, and also it even records and picks up sound.

EPOCH: the legendary Swordsman of Time; a grim young warrior sworn to serve justice for all.

BOGEY: Royal Guardian Army term for any position or vantage point.

HYRADIANS: a fascist, politically corrupt race of humans whose sole purpose is total power

and control of all they encounter. They're not above using coersion, terror, and all-out warfare to

achieve their aims.

REALM OF THE TIME BEYOND TIME: the alternate universe combining elements of the

Past and Present. For the most part, it is devoid of warfare, though it has dealt with many

invasions...and always prevailing.

FOXTROT TIME WORKS: a technologically advanced factory designed to keep the physical

forces of the Time Beyond Time from colliding with one another. There have been many

supervisors since the Works was built; the current of these is Steve Hackett, a former college

student and musician.

PROG-ROCK: a type of rock music first heard in the 1970s. This genre fuses elements of jazz,

blues, Eastern music, and science fiction concepts. This was the music played by Skywatcher's

father during his college days. (Prime examples of prog-rock are Pink Floyd, Genesis, and later,

the Alan Parsons Project.)

Union of the Life-Blades

The Chronicles of Diamond Flame and Red Ice

Book One

NOTE ON THE TEXT

This is revised and expanded version of the original 2010 text. Formatting, punctuation, and the removal and adding of words reflect these changes, done at the author's discretion.

For untold Centuries upon Centuries, the women of the Known Universe have been relegated to the role that men, in their inadvertant short-sightedness, have deemed "the fairer sex". Indeed, there are less than a few tales of the true heroism that women displayed without their due proper credit. Only in our own recent history has this been rectified. In both story and song, women have been highly glorified. Names such as Joan of Arc, Molly Pitcher, Harriet Tubman, Rosie the Riveter, Amelia Earhart, and Sally Ride are but a few examples of those whose inner goodness and purity have helped shape Mankind's history.

This is true also in the Realm of the Time Beyond Time, with names such as Adele, Skywatcher... and now we can also add the daring beautatious duo whose deeds are only now being known and recorded. They are, and will be, known for all Time as Diamond Flame; tall, blond, strongly assured of herself. At her side is her long-time friend and compatriot, the slightly diminutive Red Ice; crimson of hair, wise, humorous, yet always up for a challenge.

Together, this oddly-paired duo would rewrite the Annals of the Time Beyond Time. Evil ones had best be on their toes...

CHAPTER ONE

*"Oh, yes, I am wise but with wisdom comes the pain; yes, I've paid the price, but look how much
I've gained. If I had to, I can do anything; I am strong,invincible, I am woman . . ."*

Helen Reddy "I Am Woman" from **I Am Woman**, 1971

From the Journals of Diamond Flame:

It still strikes us as odd as to how we got mixed up in this weird yet noble Destiny. Let me tell
you, it definitely *wasn't* in our planned outcomes for the future.

And what *were* those plans?

Well, we'd just arrived at LAX from San Francisco in order to attend a conference on advanced
paramedic techniques. It was supposed to be a short, routine stay, plus it'd give us a chance to
see a couple of old friends of ours. All routine, we thought to ourselves.

Ha! That, long down the road, was to be the biggest laugh in our histories.

Where was I? Hmmm … oh yeah. Our little adventure.

(Oh, before I forget my manners, let me introduce myself. My real name's Gail McCormack, but
I'm now known as Diamond Flame. My friend you'll meet later on . . . but I'm digressing here a
bit, huh?)

After we landed at LAX and made our way to one of the finest hotels in all of L.A. we checked

in, got our room and, having entered said room, unpacked our wardrobe and finally sat down to

rest. I don't know about you but those red-eye flights from Frisco can really tire us out. Man

alive, I really dread them.

Within a few hours or so we went back downstairs to the lobby, where there congregated a flock

of paramedics from all over the States. Amongst them were a trio from La Jolla; really

young-looking. They couldn't have been more than 14 years old, at that. Later we found out,

amusingly enough, that they were part of L.A. County's "Young Paramedics" program started

up by Drs. Brackett and Early at Rampart Emergency Hospital, where the mother of one of the

pre-teen paramedics worked as a nurse. And . . . they, those young paramedics, were no older

that 12 years old. At least they were at that time, anyway.

(I know, I know . . . but it's just that so much has happened that I have to tell you about it as

logically as I can, given the circumstances.)

Returning now to our story:

After we made our intros to our fellow paramedics, we took our assigned seats and then, let the

sleepiness begin. God, I hate lectures…and I'm sure everyone else does, too. Even those kid

paramedics got restless and bored. But then again, I've never known any lecture to be dazzlingly

entertaining.

When that god-awful lecture finally ended, and we said our good nights and so-longs, my friend and I returned to our hotel suite for a pleasant night's sleep.

I can tell you right now, it would be anything *but* pleasant.

(I'll let my friend relate our tale from here in on.)

Here we meet Red Ice; she now tells her story:

Well … here I am. Not sure where to begin, but at least I can introduce myself. Then we'll go from there, okay?

My real name is Lori Lanihan. I have short close-cropped red hair, stand approximately 5 feet, 5 ½ inches, and I have blue eyes. I'm also not the type to take anything too seriously. At least, not at first.

But much to our own surprised chagrin, *that* would soon change.

How it happened was like this: after Gail and I left the hotel lobby following the lecture which we all dreadfully sat through, we returned to our room, took turns showering, dressed in our pajamas, and laid down on our beds. Somewhat lethargically, Gail turned on the television set, and ended up just surfing through one TV channel after another. I don't know about you, but I *hate* it when people do that.

I became really irritated by this.

"Gail, please find *something* to watch. Anything," I moaned.

She turned to be with a slightly pained look.

"I'm trying but there's nothing on *to* watch," she responded.

"Then try to go to sleep."

"Oh, all right," she wearily moaned out.

Big mistake!!

CHAPTER TWO

From the Journals of Diamond Flame:

We were awakened by a strange, shrillish, whining sound. It reminded me of one those alleged "emergency" signals that every TV station sends out to supposedly "test" their EBS systems.

Lori and I, not totally coherent still, turned and looked at one another.

"Hey Gail, you know what that is?" asked Lori trepidly.

I shook my head no. I knew even less than she did.

For a few minutes after that we just stood there, dumbfounded. Then ... the *real* surprise! You see, we suddenly came face-to-face with a middle-aged woman bathed in a glowing light, kind of like in *Star Wars*. She was medium to tall, with greyish-blond hair, blue-green eyes, had a petite nose, and a friendly smile on her face. There was not one wrinkle on her. She was also clad in a plain white seamless robe. I remembered seeing someone like her before, like maybe at Rampart Hospital or something.

Of course! Now I'm sure of it! It's our friend Dixie, head nurse at Rampart.

But how did she get here? And why was she glowing with that strange light around her in that weird way?

As if in reply to my questions, the woman-who-looked-like-Dixie chuckled slightly. Her smile never wavered.

"Dixie?" we mouthed silently.

She shook her head in a slight joking manner.

"No, I'm not really your friend Dixie," she said as if we uttered it out loud. *"I just happen to look like her. It'll make what I have to say to you two lucky ladies a whole lot easier."*

I regained some of my temporarily lost courage.

"If you're not our friend Dixie, then who *are* you?" I asked.

"Well, if I told you, you'd more than likely think that I was crazy or some such notion. But just out of good manners, I'll tell you anyway." And she told us her actual name which, unfortunately for you people reading this, is very unpronounceable, much less printable. Somehow, she sensed that and said for us to call her Dixie, if it suited us. It sure did, believe me.

Now…on to the purpose of Dixie's visit.

"The reason I'm here is to give you girls something you've never, ever experienced," she stated. *"But before I do this, you must swear on your lives never to reveal any of this to your friends or families."*

Shrugging our shoulders, we nodded our heads in agreement of her vow.

Then Dixie, getting her confirmation from us, did something we'd never in a million years expected *anyone* to do: she spread her arms sideways, sending forth a combination of bright light and gray powder of some sort or other.

And *that*, I dare say, was the last time we would spend in "our" world …

CHAPTER THREE

Here Red Ice takes up some more of the story:

The first thing I remember upon waking up was a cold wind blowing around us as loud as it could go. Although I was still somewhat groggy, I stood up and looked around.

And man, what sight did *I* see!

Frantically I turned to where Gail was still lying.

"Hey Gail!! Wake up!! You've gotta see *this!!*"

Slowly Gail rose up and was met by the same sight I'd just seen.

And what did we see, you ask?

Well, for starters, there was the matter of our clothes. Gail was decked out in a long suede-colored midi-skirt and matching lace-up boots, while I found myself wearing a leather one-piece tanktop/mini-skirt outfit with complementary strap-on sandals.

Then -- and this one's a doozy, people --the next thing we saw was a really weird skyline just over the horizon. There was a castle of some kind, like out of Tolkien's books in a way. Next to that a modern factory lay almost literally down the street, which was ever weirder yet. But no doubt the *strangest* of all was the sky itself.

It looked like one of those "psychedelic" paintings you see on books nowadays. The colors were an odd mix of greens, purples, blacks, oranges, and even a few we'd never seen before. Wait, there's more. There were also moons, stars, planets, and what looked like those "black holes" that they talk about on television today.

All these things added up to one question: *where are we?*

Then as if in answer, that now-familiar voice called out to us.

"Hi girls. Glad to see you're awake." It was Dixie.

We turned to her, shock registering on our faces.

"Say, Dixie, where exactly *are* we?" I asked.

"You're now in what we call the Realm of the Time Beyond Time," she said in assured confidence of herself.

Gail, being the type of girl she was, eyed her skeptically.

"Did you say -- the Time *Beyond* Time?!" Gail asked.

"Yep, I sure did."

Oh, wow, man!! Oh . . . wow!

From the Journals of Diamond Flame:

We couldn't believe what Dixie told in regards to our locale.

"And uh, where exactly *is* this Realm, I wonder?" I said.

That smile never left Dixie's face.

"Well, it's nowhere in your *universe, I can say that."*

Then a new thought quickly entered my mind.

"Now, what about our new dresses?"

A look of discovery suddenly crossed Dixie's face.

"Oh, those new outfits you have on. You see, these new dresses of yours will match your new locale . . . as well as your new Destiny."

Lori gave her a look of total befuddlement.

"New Destiny?! What new Destiny?" she asked.

"That's right. You see, your new Destiny is to help protect our Realm from harm, much as you did as San Francisco paramedics to keep people from death and suffering. So it's not all the more different." Again she kept that lovely nurse-like smile on her ageless face.

We two, Lori and I, shrugged our shoulders in resignation.

"Okay," I said, "when do we start?"

Dixie's eyes twinkled.

"Right now, so hold out your hands, girls."

So we did, and once again we were bathed in that weird *Star Wars*-like aura for what was only a few seconds. When those few seconds finally elapsed, our eyes were met by what looked like medieval swords, only they were light as feathers. The one I had was a long diamond blade, totally unblemished, ending at a solid gold hilt. Lori's blade was a more rounded ruby blade in

an onyx-and-amethyst hilt.

I had to admit right now, we were *impressed!!*

Then Dixie spoke to us again.

"These blades I've given are a reflection of your new Destinies. You, Gail McCormack, are now

and for all Time known as -- Diamond Flame." Then she turned to Lori. *"And you, Lori*

Lanihan, I now name -- Red Ice. Now . . . use these blades only to aid, not to kill. I do hope I'm

understood on this."

Oddly enough, in spite of it all . . . we understood.

CHAPTER FOUR

Here Red Ice tells more of her story:

I tell you right now, I just couldn't believe it when Dixie told us what she said about some noble

Destiny. Right now, that's the furthest thing from my mind because it just dawned on us that it

was *freezing!!* I turned back to Gail -- excuse me, Diamond Flame, raising my eyebrows to

signal her. Fortunately she got the message.

Swiftly we found an inn/hotel that seemed right out of that one British television show I like,

complete with a waiter/luggage guy who barely spoke English, and the owner wasn't that much

better. He was smarmy, crass, rude, and just plain nutty. In spite of it all, though, we giggled

ourselves silly. I mean, what would *you* do in these circumstances?

A few minutes after we checked in, we entered our rather less-than-Tolkienesque room. In fact,

it was like any hotel back home in Frisco, or even in L.A., complete with a dresser and mirror. It

seemed -- I don't know -- maybe a tad *dull.*

What happened to Gail after all this was anything *but* dull.

And why is that, you ask?

Well, Gail turned briefly to look in the mirror -- and got one hell of a surprise!! You see, she noticed something very . . . *odd* growing out from her shoulders. I can see the sudden nausea on Gail's -- I mean -- Diamond Flame's face.

There, from out of her shoulders . . . *oh my dear God!!*

Diamond Flame had sprouted -- *giant wings!!*

From the Journals of Diamond Flame:

Like Red Ice just finished saying, I did indeed get one doozy of a shock. How often does a woman go to a convention, get teleported to some other Realm or other, and just sprout gigantic -- *wings?!!* The answer: never in your lifetime, I can say that much.

I felt like I was going to throw up by then. But out of the clear blue, I heard Dixie's voice call out to us.

"Hi there again."

Swiftly I turned to her, with a combined look of fear and nausea.

"Dixie, what's *happened* to me?!"

She gave me her trademark "aha!" look of response.

"Oh, the wings. I almost neglected to tell you, Gail, that, well -- how am I going to say this? -- you're not exactly . . . human."

"You're kidding me, right?" asked Red Ice behind me.

"Nope. I'm dead serious."

I then grew *really* ticked off.

 "WHAT?!!?" I screeched, not without a dose of fear. I mean, what the hell's my husband going to think of all this?

Dixie gave us that particular look and smiled.

"Oh, I know what you're thinking. But let me say to you now, Gail, that you're a descendant of a Noble Race of female warrior/priestesses called the Startians. They're dedicated to helping people in trouble. In fact, not too long ago we just had a young Startian girl aid the Realm in warding off a deadly invading army. I think her name was -- Skywatcher. She was a really nice kid. Her dad's the top supervisor of our lone factory, and he's also a top-notch rock musician. Has been since college, as near as I can tell. But I'm getting just a little off-track here, huh?"

An odd look crossed our faces. *Skywatcher*, she said. Hmmm . . .

Dixie suddenly regained her thoughts, to her own visibly palpable relief.

"Oh, getting back to my original train of thought . . . as I was saying to you, Gail, you are of a Noble Race, unbeknownst to you on your world. I assume you know by now The Time Beyond Time doesn't exist in your universe."

"Yeah, that much we know already," said Red Ice.

"Well, it's the same with the Startians. Only you *didn't know this until you arrived here,"* said Dixie back to me. *"So I wouldn't be too concerned about it."*

She wouldn't be concerned. What about *me?!*

We'd soon find out that my -- *change* would be the least of all our worries . . .

CHAPTER FIVE

"You can bend but never break me, 'cause it'd only serve to make me more determined to achieve my final goal..."

Helen Reddy, "I Am Woman" from **I Am Woman**,1971

From the Journals of Diamond Flame:

I was still reeling a bit after Dixie told me about my totally brand new "heritage," as it were. I mean, could you believe it? Me, a born Californian, trained paramedic, now soon-to-be epic heroine from a race of Amazonian bird-women? Makes your head spin, doesn't it?

Frenzily I turned to Lori—excuse me, Red Ice.

"Why don't you *do* something, huh?"

She shrugged her shoulders.

"What do you want *me* to do?" she asked helplessly.

"I don't know. Uh, offer support, call my attorney, *just do something!! Anything!!!"* I screeched angrily.

There was a tense pause for maybe a few seconds.

"Uh, Diamond Flame?" asked Red Ice.

"What is it?" I sighed heavily

"Well, there's one small thing. I don't even know your attorney's phone number. I mean, I never really met the guy."

I couldn't help but laugh at that one.

"Red Ice, you just did me a great service."

She smiled back.

"Thanks, Diamond Flame."

"Oh, hey, you're welcome," I replied in gratitude.

Now Red Ice tells more of her story:

Well, I guess all I can add is that after I got Diamond Flame somewhat calmed down, we heard more of Dixie's rules and regulations concerning our purpose in being here in this -- what was it again? -- the Time Beyond Time, that's it. Boy, I have a hard time remembering all of that. I don't know how *anyone* does, to be honest with you.

But . . . getting back to my own original thought, Dixie, as I just said, laid down some more ground rules.

"First of all, you know not *to use your blades to harm anyone, right?"* she asked, just to make sure we got the hint.

We nodded our heads assertively. Of course we'd gotten it; after all, we are, or rather *were* paramedics.

Okay, that's fine. Now, basically it all adds up to the one simple result of your being here. And that is to keep our Realm safe, secure, happy, and bliss, which leads up back to Rule Number 1. No killing!!"

A funny -- meaning strange, not ha-ha, of course -- entered my mind.

"Uh, Dixie, if we're not allowed to kill -- and not that we'd want to, anyway -- why on Earth do we have these swords?" I asked.

That trademark "aha!" look crossed Dixie's face once again.

"Oh!! I almost forgot about that! Your swords are different than that of most other types. See, they're imbued with a power not readily seen in your universe. In a sense, they're a lot like those

laser swords in the Star Wars *movie. They can do all kinds of amazing things . . . except slice through things.*" Then she got really serious. "*And you're going to need them, believe me on that.*"

Next it was Diamond Flame's turn to ask Dixie a question.

"And why's that, Dixie?" she asked.

Dixie paused, as if she didn't want to answer.

"*Well . . . all I can say is that there's going to be trouble. Bad trouble. So be on guard, be brave, and most of all, don't be killers!! Got it?*"

"We got it," we said in unison.

Only we didn't know just how bad this trouble would be!

CHAPTER SIX

From the Journals of Diamond Flame:

For day after day we waited and waited for any sign of this "bad trouble" that Dixie warned us about. I don't know about you but my already-shaky nerves were just about shot to blazes. I mean, how much more of this weirdness can we take?

Even Red Ice, as normally easy-going as she was, felt the bite of that certain, uh -- *uncertainty.* And unlike me, she let her feelings be known.

"Hey, Diamond Flame? What'll happen, I wonder?" she asked.

"I don't know, but what I *do* know is that I'm not looking forward to it at all in the slightest bit," I replied, inadvertantly letting my inner fear creep to the surface.

Then her eyes clouded over, her lips quvering. God, she was really frightened out of her mind. And I do mean, *frightened.*

I turned to her and held her tightly, like a mother hen, in a way.

It did little to calm her fears and anxieties, if anything at all.

Here Red Ice relates more of her tale:

As Diamond Flame just finished telling you guys, I really got all-out panicky and nervous just waiting for God-knows-what kind of trouble that might come at any moment now. I mean, this isn't what I was trained to do, and it certainly ain't exactly my life's calling now, was it?

From that second on, my stomach and nerves held a fast-paced contest to see which would drive me insane first. I can tell you now that *this* little contest would end in a tie. Either way, of course, *I'd* come out the loser. And I can assure you now that Diamond Flame's nerves were equally as shot as mine were.

Of course, she'd never admit that to *your* face. She'd never hear the end of it if she did. Tell you, that is to say. But then again, that's Diamond Flame for you.

Anyway, the waiting and waiting drove all of us nuts. I mean, just what or *who* are we expected to fight, anyhow? Our in-laws? The President? *Kermit the Frog and Miss Piggy?!* Gimme an answer, will you?

Oh, all right. I'll let the events come as they come, so to speak.

Aw, %$!!#!!! *Now* where was I at in my story? Hmmm . . . oh yeah.

Well, as near as I can figure in spite of the growing fear that ate us up like cheap chicken burritos, we also felt a sense of -- I don't know -- *electric excitement!* Yeah, that's it. *That's* what it was. A great feeling of it, too.

But, as with anything else in life, that feeling wasn't gonna last much longer.

From the Journals of Diamond Flame:

Yeah, I had to admit I *did* feel a sense of excitement in my bones. I mean, how often do you get to take part in a grand adventure where you, and your best friend, have the chance to actually *change* the course of universal destiny? Gloria Steinhem and Helen Reddy, eat your hearts out!

But of course, as the old saying goes, "Be careful what you wish for, because you very well might get it." And boy, did *that* become pertinent much later on . . .

CHAPTER SEVEN

Red Ice relates some more of the story:

I was sweating out buckets as the moments before zero hour ran by like Bruce Jenner after he ate

6,295 bowls of his Wheaties. With lots of extra sugar, of course. Unfortunately, those racing

moments also ate my calm reserve up as well as induced me to start eating my fingernails. And

let me tell you people now, I *hate* the taste of my own fingernails . . . especially if they've been

polished! Yecchh!! Ugh! Makes me cringe!!

Anyway, we were getting really antsy about the events that would soon happen to us as well as

the entire -- what was it again? -- the Realm of the Time Beyond Time, that's it. God, I still can't

remember all of that even now. I don't know how *you* do it.

Gail -- I mean, Diamond Flame, on the other hand, grew oddly . . . *serene* about the whole thing.

Oh well, that's modernist feminism for you, I guess.

From the Journals of Diamond Flame:

I felt a growing sense of serene resolve in my being as time moved onwards to wherever it goes,

be it in the Present or, into the Future. In fact, I couldn't wait to begin the fight to help the Noble

Beings of the Time Beyond Time, like Dixie told us about before. It's as if my old life was

somehow . . . gradually fading into the deepest recesses of my mind. I was more than ready to welcome it. I realized now that *this* is what I really wanted in life, though I couldn't speak for Red Ice in this instance.

In fact, I was even getting to the point where I didn't *want* to go back to my husband and kids. Truth be known to you, I thought my husband was a bit of a chauvanistic Neanderthal, even in spite of the fact that he was a professor of sociology at UCSB. And my kids -- well, they were typical, normal, and downright *demanding!* I wouldn't wish that on my worst enemy -- well, maybe I would, in the new grand scheme of things, as it were.

But . . . oh, I'm digressing big time here, aren't I?

Getting back on track, Red Ice and I kept on waiting and waiting, with Dixie always at our side, guiding us along as we needed it. And let me tell you, we sure did need it!

Red Ice relates more of her story:

I don't know what Diamond Flame told you folks, but I've got to say now that I got a very weird feeling in my gut, although I couldn't place my finger on it . . . yet. But I *do* know that somehow I definitely would *not* like it one iota. Ahh, maybe I'm just paranoid or something, I don't know.

Anyhow, we kept an increasingly tense vigil for whatever kind of "bad trouble" that Dixie had warned us about shortly after we arrived here. In fact, I turned to Dixie to tell her my feelings on the subject. I mean, she *did* teleport us here, right?

"Uh, Dixie, can I talk to you for a bit?" I asked.

She turned casually to me with that luminescent look that was ever so prevalant on her ageless face, her smile never leaving.

"Yeah, sure, Red Ice, what's on your mind?"

I made no hesitation in replying.

"Hey, Dixie, did you sense some kind of . . . *change* coming over Gail, I mean, Diamond Flame? It's as if she's not -- I don't know -- *herself.* And to be honest, I'm getting more than a little nervous."

Then, for the first time, Dixie's smile somewhat . . . *faded.*

"Yeah, I see what you mean," she said, turning her gaze to Diamond Flame.

Instantly my nerves grew really shaky at that point!

CHAPTER EIGHT

From the Journals of Diamond Flame:

I could sense Red Ice's growing anxiety about the events that we kept on waiting and waiting for. My "old" life was increasingly growing blurry and indistinct, as if I was waking up from some awfully batty dream that I had before I "awoke." And I can't even begin to try to tell you about the joy that was also increasing in my gut.

Or maybe that my "new life" was making Red Ice nervous. I mean, I had noticed her growing jumpiness of late, and it worried the hell out of me by this stage.

Then I saw Red Ice walk up to me, that worried-rabbit look etched on her face. She must have talked to Dixie beforehand.

"Hey Diamond Flame, we need to talk. Now!" she stated tensely.

I eyed her rather funnily.

"Uh, sure. okay. Let's talk," I replied.

Swiftly she got right to the point.

"Listen, I don't know what's happening to you, but I definitely don't like it one bit. I'm not sure if you're aware of it or not but quite honestly, you're starting to scare the living *hell* out of me. You understand what I'm getting at?"

"To be blunt with you, Red Ice . . . no, I don't," I answered rather testily.

Then she eyed me in a very angry manner. *That* I didn't like.

"Well, if that's how you want it, fine with me." She then stormed away, teary-eyed and quite hurt.

Dismissively I shook my head, as if to clear my thoughts. She'll get over it. Just a little scared of everything, that's all.

No big deal, I thought -- well, I hoped . . .

Red Ice tells more of her thoughts:

After a few minutes to myself, I calmed down and my old light-heartedness returned, allowing my feelings to get back to normal. I mean, I could just kick myself for reacting the way that I did in regards to Diamond Flame's new attitude. I can't blame her, really.

I mean, we didn't exactly *ask* to come here, but what are you gonna do?

It was at that exact moment that Diamond Flame walked over to me.

"Hey. I want to apologize to you. It's just that -- well, to be honest with you, I'm beginning to adjust and even *enjoy* this new life here. I didn't mean to hurt you like I did, and for that I truly am sorry. You forgive me, Red Ice?"

I couldn't help but smile at her. Like I always do when things are okay.

"Ahh, what the hell. You're forgiven." And like a good kid sister I embraced the teddy-bear stuffings out of her, crying in joy.

Now that *that's* overwith, we got back to worrying about the supposed "bad trouble" that Dixie kept on repeating about.

That, we soon realized, would come a hell of a lot sooner than expected.

CHAPTER NINE

From the Journals of Diamond Flame:

After Red Ice calmed down, and forgave me for my new outlook, we then set upon the task of learning how to use our blades, with good old Dixie supervising us along the way, amazed by us for our increasingly expert-like adaptability in our usage.

"Okay, let's start with you, Diamond Flame," she said, turning to me. *"You see that withered-up old oak tree over there?"*

"Yes, I do."

"All right, just swing your blade like you would swing a baseball bat at a ball game, and watch what happens afterwards."

"Okay, here goes nothing." And with that, I did as Dixie instructed, and I've gotta tell you now, I was not only impressed but also *awestruck!* You see, the moment I did that, that old tree actually compressed itself, and then -- *ka-thooom!!* It exploded in a blinding burst of light that could've been seen for miles around. In fact, I think I even saw Red Ice's jaw drop like a brick falling from a high building!

As did mine!

Now Red Ice tells us the results of her instruction:

All I could say about Diamond Flame's power is "Oh my God!!" I mean, it was really impressive to see what she accomplished. Then Dixie turned to me.

"Now it's your turn, Red Ice." She pointed to another old oak tree, all barren and more wrinkled than my old high school prom dress. *"Point the blade at the tree, lift it up very slowly, and then swing downward as hard as you can, and watch the results."*

"Well . . . okay." Presently I follow Dixie's instructions, and as impressed as I was with Diamond Flame's power test, mine was even more jaw-dropping. Why, you ask? Well, see, what happened was that...well, try to imagine an old, wrinkly tree just lifting itself off the ground like a helium balloon, and then, as it freezes up in mid-flight -- come *crashing* down to Earth, just literally shattering to a quazillion fragments never to be seen again! At least, not in *this* lifetime, anyway.

"Like, wow, Dixie, that was *dynamite!!*" I yelled in surprised triumph.

Diamond Flame was as impressed as I was. Maybe more so.

"I didn't know you had it in you, Red Ice," she said, still in awe.

"You know what? I didn't, either," I replied, smiling broadly.

Then Dixie turned to both of us.

*"Well, girls, I must say that you've both impressed me to no end. That shows you've got strength and power which, to be quite honest, wasn't allowed to come out on your world, thanks to centuries of historical short-sightedness if not short-*mindedness. *I'm proud for both of you. This all means that now you're ready and more than capable of deterring the Danger that's going to come to us real soon."*

As usual, our collective curiosity got piqued. It was also mixed with more than a twinge of fear and worry.

"Hey Dixie, what exactly is this 'Danger' you keep mentioning to us?" I asked.

Unbelievably, her usual smile faded completely from her face.

"Well, I can't tell you right away but all I can *reveal is that it has to do with someone who you might know in your world as a nice guy, but now, in the Realm, is out for power if not bloodshed."*

Then we actually saw *tears* roll down her face.

CHAPTER TEN

From the Journals of Diamond Flame:

Day after day we improved our sword-wielding skills, getting increasingly adept at it. It was as if we -- well, you get the idea. I know Red Ice got the idea. And … she began to show her new resolve more and more as time went on. Yet we couldn't shake that ominous thought Dixie planted on our minds in regards to our opponent. I mean, it really terrified the hell out of us.

Unexpectedly Dixie came up to us, still having that worried look on her face.

"Hey Dixie, you okay?" asked Red Ice.

Dixie didn't readily answer at first. It's as if she needed to weigh out her words.

"Yeah, I'm okay. Just thinking," she finally replied.

"About what, Dixie?" I questioned.

"Oh, about your enemy, that's all. And I don't mind telling you girls now that he won't be a pushover. In fact, I think it's time I told you who it is you're going to be combatting in the moments to come."

Our eyes boggled out in shock mixed with curiosity.

"Well, who *is* it, Dixie?" asked Red Ice, who tended to be a bit impatient.

Dixie pursed her lips and carefully thought out her decision to tell us.

"Well, you girls know your friend Dr. Brackett at Rampart Hospital, right?"

We nodded our heads in reply.

"Well, in our *Realm, the one you know as Dr. Brackett has an evil doppelganger, or twin brother named Robrack --"* began Dixie.

Robrack!!! Oh my God!!

Here Red Ice takes up the tale some more:

I stopped Dixie right there!

"Wait a minute, Dixie. Did you say -- *Robrack?!"* I asked in frightened confusion.

Dixie nodded somberly.

"So!! *Now* we get it. You mention the name Skywatcher, right?" asked Diamond Flame in sudden realization.

Again Dixie nodded in that sad manner.

"Hey, Diamond Flame!! You realize we're going to fight the enemy of Skywatcher?! Of course!" I yelled out.

"Yeah, that's right, huh?" replied Diamond Flame. "But I thought that was only a science fiction tale I read to my kids."

"Well, it actually happened not too long ago, I can assure you of that now," said Dixie, her smile and light-hearted strength returning to her.

I had a thought in my head just then.

"But, Dixie, didn't he get his butt shipped on outta here at the end of the saga?"

"Well, yes he did but like any insidious villain, he managed to escape, and now he wants all-out revenge on the entire Realm. And ... he doesn't care who gets hurt, as long as he gains his vengeance. So, be on your toes at all times, girls . . . and be brave and strong for all of us," she told us.

Diamond Flame smiled in supreme confidence.

"Oh, don't worry, Dixie. If he tries anything sneaky, we'll have his behind for a lunch buffet,"
she said rather rashly.

It was then that Dixie eyed us in an almost angry manner.

"I wouldn't take him so lightly if I were you two. Remember, he's from a race of militaristic
fascists, and though he was defeated once he'll keep coming back for more. In a sense, he's a
glutton for punishment -- provided it's he who dishes it out."

Another thought popped into my head.

"If what you're saying is true, then why didn't you summon Skywatcher instead of coming to us
in order to deal with Robrack?" I asked.

"Well . . ." stated Dixie, *"see, Skywatcher left the Realm in order to further her cause for Justice*
for all the Noble Beings. Plus, she's not the young teenage girl that you read about. She's a
full-grown woman now, and probably wants nothing to do with Robrack."

Aha! *Now* we got the message. At least, we hoped . . .

CHAPTER ELEVEN

From the Journals of Diamond Flame:

Now that we'd gotten the idea of who our foe was, all that remained now was to wait for him to make his move. Knowing these types of villains and how they operate, *that* would not be long in coming! As I keep saying to you people, it's all a matter of time . . .

From out of the blue sky, we suddenly heard a low, chopping sound echo all around us. We turned to look and lo and behold . . . *there he was!! In all his unwelcome glory!! Robrack's airship!!*

Red Ice's boggled in confusion.

"Hey, wait a second here! I thought that his airship was destroyed when Skywatcher threw soapy water on the control-panel," she said to Dixie, recalling the story that we'd both read.

"Yeah. That's right, Dixie," I said in agreement.

"Well, you've gotta hand it to these villains -- they're resourceful. They always have back-ups of everything. Weapons, money, henchmen, you name it, they have it in spades. And always ready to confound us heroine-types," replied Dixie, not without some anger.

We looked at each other in utter bewilderment, shaking our heads.

Red Ice, as usual, picks up where Diamond Flame left off:

I don't know about the rest of you, but I was very much ready to kick Robrack's behind back to wherever he managed to escape from. I'm sure Diamond Flame felt the exact same way. In fact, I *know* she felt that way, believe me on that.

Swiftly my new steel nerve was vibrating with electric anticipation in regards to our mission -- no, make that our new life's calling. God, I couldn't wait.

I wanted to do it *now!!* And I, of course, told all this to Dixie.

Not surprisingly, she gently chewed me out.

"Well, Red Ice, you're just going to have *to wait, that's all. I know you're excited to fight Robrack off, but that excitement* could *be your undoing if you're not careful. So try your best to remain patient, and also try to keep* some *sense of logic about all of this, okay?"* Then her smile returned in full force. *"Besides,"* she continued, *"that wasn't* really *Robrack's airship you heard. That was a cheap sound effect I created to test out your alertness. You passed, of course, but you've* still *got to be* patient. *I do hope I'm clear on that."*

"Oh, yeah, you're real clear on that," I replied brightly. "But what about the airship we actually

saw?"

That goofy yet loving look also returned with a vengeance.

"Oh, that!! Just another cheap illusion, that's all. You know, special effects and such."

Of course. Somehow I wasn't the least bit surprised, considering all we've seen . . .

CHAPTER TWELVE

From the Journals of Diamond Flame:

I had to hand it to Dixie; she really kept us on our toes just so when the moment actually *did* arrive, we'd be definitely more than ready for Robrack and his plots. I don't know what we'd do without her guidance…and I sure as hell didn't want to find out, either.

But somewhere in the recesses of my mind, we knew that the time would come when Dixie *wouldn't* be there to help us along. Yet in an odd sense, I was rather looking forward to that challenge. I mean, I've faced them all my life. I got challenged by my parents when I told them of my desire to join the SFFD as a paramedic; they told me that I was crazy for considering such an idea.

Then, of course, my husband laughed at me when I told him the same thing. He said, in his educated chauvanist manner, that women have no business in the fire department. Inside, I wanted to kick his ass for even *thinking* such a remark, much less actually saying it out loud to my face! No wonder, then, that I didn't want to go back to my "old" life.

I just hope I could get Red Ice to understand all of this . . .

As usual by now, Red Ice takes up the slack in our tale:

In spite of how I felt and reacted earlier, I grew just as serene as Diamond Flame in my own confidence. In fact, it even allowed my impatience to sail away into the deep recesses of my mind, replacing it with a good deal of wisdom. I mean, I wasn't as militaristically feminist as she was, but I *did* remember my own boyfriend, who, as much as I love him, could be a bit of a jackass at times.

But . . . yeah, I know. Back to the story at hand.

On our own initiative, we improved our sword-wielding skills moment by moment as Dixie kept watch on both us and the increasingly ominous skies above our heads. I was definitely more than up to the challenge that Dixie laid out for us. And I'm sure that Diamond Flame felt as staunch as I did.

Presently I turned to Dixie, always with a persistent question or two in my head.

"Hey, Dixie, you got any idea of when Robrack'll show his sorry ass up?"

Dixie looked at me rather inscrutably.

"I don't know when he'll show up exactly, but you can wager every last cent he'll be more than itching to have his revenge. And another thing: try not to use so much of that profanity, if you can." She really hated my choice of words. Eh, it doesn't bug me all that much -- if at all.

Right now, the only thing bugging me is not being able to face Roback down.

Sooner than we all expected, though, his ass would be here, and we'd best damn well be on our toes when he does!

CHAPTER THIRTEEN

From the Journals of Diamond Flame:

We casually walked around the grounds of the Realm, just taking everything in that we could when, unexpectedly, we heard from out of the multi-colored skies a loud, streaking *vwhoosh!!* sound echoing all around!

Swiflty we turned to Dixie, our eyes filled with a mix of excitement and curiosity.

"Hey, Dixie, did you hear that just now?!" asked Red Ice, her eyes widening.

Somberly Dixie nodded her head.

"Yep, I sure did. And I can assure you that this *time it wasn't me creating a cheap illusion. Look up again, and you'll know what I mean."*

As instructed, we did so and lo and behold again, there really *was* a giant airship, moving through the skies like the Goodyear blimp high on uppers! Presently our eyes boggled!!

"Hey Diamond Flame, don't blimps, or airships, or whatever they're called, move a lot -- *slower* than that?" Red Ice asked me, perplexed.

"Well, don't forget we're in another Realm. *Anything* can happen here," I replied.

Dixie, having overheard our conversation, made her observation known.

"Unless I miss my guess, I'd say that since Robrack escaped his imprisonment, he managed to somehow . . . upgrade his technology! You're right about airships moving slowly but knowing Robrack, he probably stole the secrets of FTL travel from another more highly advanced Realm beyond even this one!"

"FTL?!?" asked out Red Ice.

"That's 'faster than light' in case you're wondering. You know, warp-speed on *Star Trek* or hyper-drive in the *Star Wars* movie," I responded.

"Oh, I get it now!!" said Red Ice excitedly. "It's some sort of a speed-attack!"

Then the mood grew more somber by the minute!

We knew by now that we had to *move like hell!!!*

Once again Red Ice takes up her end of the story:

Well, folks, this was *it!!* Our moment to fight had arrived and I don't know about Diamond Flame or even Dixie, but I have to tell you that I was *more* than ready to kick Robrack's sorry ass back to wherever he hailed from.

I turned to Diamond Flame, my eyes blazing in delight. She somberly got the hint!

"Okay, girls, this is what you've been training and preparing for. Are you sure *you're up to this?"* Dixie asked us, not without worry.

Diamond Flame's eyes lightened in an even more intense blaze.

"Ready as hell, Dixie. Ready as hell!!" she replied, a grim smile on her face.

"And *I'm* ready as well. Ready to kick some Robrack ass!!" I gleefully said.

Somberly, almost sadly, Dixie nodded her head, as if to give us the start.

"All right . . . go kick his ass from here to wherever!"

Let's get it on, people!!

Let's get it *on!!*

CHAPTER FOURTEEN

From the Journals of Diamond Flame:

I could easily understand Red Ice's over-eagerness to fight Robrack, but I knew, from a logic standpoint, we needed a battle plan. And as such, I told this to her, partly -- well, mostly to calm her down.

"Okay, so we need a plan. What exactly *is* this plan you're trying to come up with?" she asked, rather rashly at first. Then her eyes did the Edith Bunker boggle. See, whenever Red Ice has an idea, her eyes get all googly. Frankly, I didn't like that look.

"Hey, Diamond Flame!! I've got an idea!!" she yelled.

Immediately I knew what she was thinking, but I humored her.

"And uh, just do you have in mind?" I asked even though, as I said before, I knew what she thought of.

"Well, since you've now got wings from out of your shoulders I figured that maybe you can launch a speed-attack of your own."

Oddly enough, a broad grin creased my face. Red Ice had the *perfect* idea!!

"Say no more, Red Ice. Let's do it!!"

And with that having been said I turned my gaze to the multi-colored skies, stretched my long arms outward, and thus . . . I was truly *airborne!!* Let me tell you now, folks, it was really *exhilarating!!!*

I was also to find out that it was downright *terrifying* as well . . .

As usual, Red Ice relates her thoughts:

As soon as I saw Diamond Flame rise to the sky like that, I was really impressed. In fact, I thought she looked . . . I don't know -- *beautifully graceful,* that's it. Yeah, sure!

But like Diamond Flame probably told you, I got an ominous sense of growing danger in the pit of my stomach. And once again, my nerves was almost to due be shot to hell when I heard Dixie call out to me.

"Red Ice!! Over here!!"

Swiftly I raced from my present spot to where I later saw Dixie as she was looking upwards to where Diamond Flame had literally flown.

"What is it, Dixie?" I asked, not without worry.

Her face grew more and more grim as she gazed at me.

"I just sensed something quite perilous echoing through my mind. It's as if -- " she said, not finishing her thought.

"What? What did you *see,* Dixie? Please tell me."

Without saying a word, she made me close my eyes even as she placed her hand on my forehead. All at once, a flood of thoughts and visions cascaded into my mind-- and they were downright *horrifying!!*

"What do you see, Red Ice?" she somberly asked me.

"I see…the entire Realm in flames!! Children crying and screaming!! Men and women fleeing for their lives!! I see…Robrack laughing at these things!! Homes and shops burning!! I see… *oh my GOD!! NO!!"* I screamed, as though I was in great physical pain.

"What else *do you see? Tell me!* Now!!*"* she commanded.

I didn't want to tell her, but really I didn't have too many other options.

"I see…some place called -- the *Foxtrot Time Works!!!* It's under attack!! In fact, it's -- oh, God,

NO!! NO!!! It's being destroyed!! And the entire Universe of the Realm is -- collapsing!!!"

God almighty, I was shaking and sweating out buckets. *And…*I was crying as well, considering

what I had just visioned in my mind thanks to Dixie.

"What I've just made you see is what could *happen if Robrack's ass isn't kicked and soon!!*

That's *what he wants now, in order to get his vengeance. Before that, all he wanted was control.*

Now it's all-out Destruction and massive Chaos!!"

Unable to withstand it much longer, I turned my head aside to throw up.

In her usual show of maternalistic sympathy, she embraced me even as I started crying like a

baby all over again. And I just couldn't stop the tears from rolling down…

Where's Diamond Flame when I really need her??

From the Journals of Diamond Flame:

Even though I was feeling ecstatically joyful being airborne(thanks to my new "heritage"), I had

some deep reserve about leaving Red Ice behind on land, not knowing her real part in all of this.

I mean, I really care for her, in a very meaningfully special way, if you know what I'm getting at.

But in order to fulfill at least *my* part in our mission of protecting the Realm, I was forced to put those concerns and worries on the back-burner. I had no choice on this, really. For this, Red Ice, I apologize but the battle *must* go on!!

CHAPTER FIFTEEN

Red Ice relates to us now the events of the next moments:

After Dixie calmed me down, we ran like hell to the location of . . . oh, what was it, again? The Foxtrot Time Works, that's it. I was really *amazed* by the layout. All modern and yet so "retro" at the same time (no cheap 1-cent pun intended). Unbelievably, Dixie acted like she was *not* all that impressed by it all.

She let that feeling be known by casually strolling up to the main entranceway and ringing the signal button on the outside intercom. Immediately we got a response.

"Yes?" said a clipped, precise, almost British female voice.

"Is Mr. Steve Hackett in?" asked Dixie. *"It's a matter of grave importance."*

"Who should I say is calling, please?"

*"Tell Mr. Hackett it concerns a certain old…*friend *of his,"* she stated.

"Just a second, I'll send him to you now."

Actually, we waited for more than five minutes, before the door opened. When it did, we were met by the guy we assumed to be the supervisor. He was tall, a little on the thin side, with slightly long blackish-brown hair, blue eyes that made him half-asleep; overall I thought he was cute. Then unexpectedly Dixie eyed me in a very wary manner.

Oh! I forgot to mention he wore a paisley long-sleeved shirt, dark-brown bell bottom jeans, shiny black shoes, and a leather jacket. (Did I mention that he was clean-shaven, as well?)

"Yes, may I help you?" he asked in a British accent.

"Mr. Hackett? You don't know me, but I have some very *disturbing news for you, and you're definitely not going to be pleased,"* said Dixie grimly.

He eyed us suspiciously.

"What kind of news?" he asked, even as the truth slowly dawned on him.

Dixie sighed heavily, as if she didn't want to say what she had to say.

"Mr. Hackett, you know Robrack, the arch-enemy of your daughter Skywatcher, right?" asked Dixie, even though she *knew* the answer to that one.

"Unfortunately, yes I do," he said angrily.

There was a tense pause lasting more than five minutes.

"Well, Mr. Hackett . . . he escaped his imprisonment and has now returned to exact his revenge for being defeated by your little girl. He's out for blood this time." Then she turned to me. *"You see, this young lady received a terrifyingly apocalyptic vision in regards to the Foxtrot Time Works being all-out --* eliminated!!!*"*

"And who might *you* be?" asked Mr. Hackett, turning his gaze to me.

"Oh, hi. My name's Red Ice and well, basically we just got here," I answered.

"We?" he questioned, raising his eyebrows.

"Well yeah, my friend is even now flying towards Robrack's new-and-improved airship as I stand here telling you all this."

His jaw dropped to the ground!!

"You don't mean -- ?"

I smiled impishly.

"Yep, my friend, the soon-to-be-known Diamond Flame, is actually of the same race as your wife and little girl," I said, giggling.

"How the heck do you know about us?" he queried, now in a state of shock.

Dixie eyed me warily again. I just couldn't help what came next.

"Oh, it's simple. I just . . . *read* about your adventure. Really fascinating, I thought."

Then he burst out laughing; somehow I felt we won him over.

Wait till I tell Diamond Flame *this* little bit of news!!

From the Journals of Diamond Flame:

For hour upon hour I searched relentlessly for Robrack's airship, without any real success what-so-ever. Even as my frustration mounted, I kept wondering about Red Ice and Dixie. A series of ominous thoughts entered my mind. The biggest was their safety. I mean, I have a special concern for Red Ice, what with her being younger than I and all. Feeling physically worn out, I decided to make my way back to them . . .

When I landed I was warmly greeted by Red Ice, Dixie, and someone I was sure that I read about . . . oh, yeah, that's right. It was Mr. Steve Hackett. You know, Skywatcher's dad, as if I had to remind you of that.

"Hi, gang," I said, getting a hug from Red Ice along the way.

Rapidly, Red Ice turned her gaze to Mr. Hackett.

"Oh, Mr. Hackett, this is Diamond Flame. The one I told you about," she said.

Quickly I shook his hand as if he was a slot machine in Vegas.

"Hi! So you're Skywatcher's dad, huh?"

Looking at me rather incredulously, he slowly nodded his head.

"Uhh . . .yes, that's me, all right," he replied self-deprecatingly.

Just then, Dixie ended this little introduction tersely.

"Ahem. Sorry to end this so abruptly, but there's still the matter of finding Robrack and defeating him once and for all!!"

God, were we really embarrassed by then!!

CHAPTER SIXTEEN

Red Ice, as is her usual thing, picks up the story once more:

After the palabra-dabra-ba was all settled we went to a local place called *The Last Refuge*, ordered ourselves some food and drinks provided by the owner (who, as you're going to hear now, looks exactly like Don Henley from the Eagles), and began to formally finalize our battle strategy.

My only question was: where the hell did Mr. Hackett fit in all this?

I had a feeling that I wouldn't like the answer to that. Not at all.

But it wasn't my place to question Dixie's judgement too harshly. I mean, you can't help but admire her. She cares…quite a lot.

Then not unexpectedly, Mr. Hackett got up from the table, and made his way to the door of *The Last Refuge.*

"Excuse me, ladies, but I really *must* get back to the Foxtrot Time Works. I'm on the tightest schedule imaginable, you know. Which reminds me, it's time I had a chat with one Mr. Arthur P.Q. Royal," he said, even as he was almost out the door.

"Just a minute, Steve," yelled Dixie. *"We're not done with you yet."*

Immediately he turned around and made his way back to our table.

"Maybe I didn't make myself clear. I just said I'm on a set schedule, and well, to be blunt, I don't personally care what you do with your battle plan. I've had *more* that quite enough excitement and adventure for my lifetime, and I don't need any more of that, thank you very much!" Man, was he *ever* mad!!

Dixie then did something that *was* unexpected: *she lost her temper!!!*

"Now look, you!! You best get your ass over here right now, sit down in that chair, and you damn well better LISTEN *to what we have to say!!!* IS THAT CLEAR?!!" Now we know not to get Dixie irritated for any given reason.

"You know, I'm getting a trite bit tired of repeating myself over and over. And another thing: don't *ever* raise your voice to me again. I didn't take it from my daughter, and I'm more than certainly not going to accept it from *you!!"*

Dixie eyed him, still angry as hell. Wearily she sighed.

"Okay . . . I finally see your point, Steve. You win. Go."

"Gladly, but if I ever change my mind -- and that's a pretty hefty 'if' -- you'll be the first to acknowledge that fact. Deal?" He was smiling slightly.

"Okay, it's a deal, Steve. Now you best get back to work," said Dixie, returning the smile graciously after her explosive tirade.

We couldn't believe our eyes and ears!!

From the Journals of Diamond Flame:

After seeing Mr. Hackett waltz his way out the door, I began to realize his point. I mean, he wasn't the type of guy who enjoys every adventure that comes his way…especially when it involves a great loss. Namely his only daughter -- indeed, his only child, period.

I made it a point to bring this up with Dixie.

"Hey, Dixie, did you *really* have to lose your cool like that? I mean, the man just lost his daughter," I said.

Sighing very heavily, she nodded her head in somber agreement.

"Yeah I know, Diamond Flame. But it's my duty to ensure the safety of the entire Realm of the Time Beyond Time, and I really can't let personal family issues stand in the way of my fulfilling that duty. You understand that, don't you?"

I nodded my own head. I got the message.

CHAPTER SEVENTEEN

From the Journals of Diamond Flame:

For day after day, we searched over and over for any sign of Robrack, as my own feelings on the mission grew increasingly compromised. I mean to say that even though I still enjoyed my new life here, I truly began to see Mr. Hackett's view clearly . . . if only from an advocate's mindset.

Anyway, I was constantly reminded by Dixie to keep those thoughts on the back-burner. The mission took precedence over all else at this stage in the game.

Just after the fall of night on our third day of searching, Red Ice turned to me.

"Hey Diamond Flame, can I talk to you?"

"Yeah, sure. What's on your mind?"

She paused, as if she had to measure her words carefully.

"Well . . . I don't know about you, but I got the strangest feeling in my gut just now. It's as if -- I don't know. I can't put my finger on it."

I held up my hand to stop her.

"Don't say anything more, Red Ice. Try to put it out of your mind, if you can," I told her rather sternly. "Our mission is the key thing now, okay?"

She agreed, shrugging her shoulders in the process.

"Okay, if that's how it is, that's how it is."

I hugged her tightly to soothe her troubled mind.

"It'll be okay. Promise," I vowed to her…and, of course, to whoever we're telling all this to as well.

Red Ice relates some more of our adventure, as usual:

In spite of Diamond Flame's vow to help make everything all right, that gnawing feeling never really left me. In fact, I think it grew a little worse. Of course, I didn't tell *her* that. She'd never let me hear the end of it all.

But I tried to follow her advice almost too much to the letter. She was right. We had a mission to fulfill. *And . . .* I figured the only thing to soothe my nerves was to find Robrack and kick his pompous, egotistically over-inflated ass form here to wherever-land! Yeah!

Then, on the fourth day, our moment arrived at long last! Our ears were greeted by that now-familiar *vwhooshing* sound. Swiftly we turned our gaze to the skies, and lo and behold for the third time, Robrack's hyperactive airship came into view. Then, unbelievably, it actually *slowed down!!*

All right, Mr. Robrack, you snot, now *you'll get YOURS!!!*

From the Journals of Diamond Flame:

Let me be the first to say to you that I ws really elated to see Red Ice back to her old, cheerful, confident self again. It really did us both some good, I can assure you of that fact. And it made *me* all the more ready and willing to do whatever it took to help Dixie fulfill her -- well, it's *our* mission, now, as well. There was now no way in hell that we'd dare disappoint her!

Turning back to Red Ice, I decided to lay out a variation of our original battle plan using my new-found flying ability, which by now I was more than ecstatically happy to embrace.

To echo Red Ice's thoughts…Robrack, you're ours now!

CHAPTER EIGHTEEN

From the Journals of Diamond Flame:

Red Ice walked up to me, that mischievous twinkle still in her eyes.

"So, what do you plan to do? As if I had to ask," she said.

"Well, if at first you don't succeed with your plan -- " I began to say.

"Try, try again and again," she finished.

And so, with nothing much else to lose, we resumed our now-desperate search for Robrack and

his airship that moved as if it, as Red Ice already told you people, was high on uppers.

Fortunately for little old me, *that* wouldn't any problem what-so-ever.

The problem was -- what to do with him *afterwards . . .*

Now an old "friend" of ours interrupts to relate his side of our tale -- unfortunately:

Well, hello again, you goody-goodies. Yes, it's me. "Good" old Robrack here, back to wreak

even more devastation and havoc for your reading pleasure. I don't know about you, and I'm not

at all certain about the future, as if I actually care anyway, but it's good to be here once more.

(Well, maybe there *is* one thing that I do care about. And I'm sure you know what it is, right? I say again, right? Yeah, sure you do. Just don't go around actually *saying* that brat's name.)

But getting back to my more rational train of thought, I laid out my plans of not taking control of the Foxtrot Time Works, but actually *laying it to total waste and ruin!!!!*

And I'll bet you people reading all this are wondering why.

The answer's simple, folks: *revenge!* Plain and simple!!

Only this time, no bird-brained busty Amazon would even dare *think* to stop me now!!

Once more Red Ice takes up where Diamond Flame left off:

Diamond Flame looked up to the skies, just staring at Robrack's huge airship hovering over our heads. She had a very peculiar expression on her now-pale face. It's as if she felt a twinge of grim satisfaction or something, I don't know. And frankly, it chilled the hell out of me. Wouldn't *you* feel that way if you were me?

Presently she walked to where I stood, that same grim look on her face.

"We need to talk. Now," she stated.

"Sure, okay," I replied, shrugging my shoulders.

We walked to a small hill just a few feet from the main town. A weird sense overwhelmed me by then.

"I want to tell you something that I dare not say in front of Dixie," she said.

"And, uh, what's that?"

Before she actually answered me, she put her hands on my shoulders and just *stared* somberly into my eyes. If anything, her expression grew more grimmer by the minute, if that was at all possible.

"I might not come back from this mission alive," she flatly said.

My jaw dropped like a brick!!

"*What?!?*" I couldn't *believe* it!!

"That's right, Red Ice. I'll more than likely die before this is all done. I can feel it in my bones, in my soul."

"Diamond Flame, that's just plain *crazy!!*"

She nodded her head in agreement, but didn't dispute her own sad resolve...

From the Journals of Diamond Flame:

I didn't feel all that thrilled about telling my darkest thought to Red Ice, but out of my love and concern for her, and for the sake of honesty in general, I *had* to tell her. Otherwise, I wouldn't be able to live with myself.

"Live with myself." An odd phrase, I thought. Very odd, indeed . . .

Red Ice lets her *darkest thoughts be known:*

God almighty, I was still shocked by what Diamond Flame told you guys. I mean, what the hell is she *planning?!* Suicide, or what??

At that moment I really let her have it from me!

"Hey!! Listen, I don't know what went wrong with you, but you know what? You've got a hell of a lot to live for!! I mean, you've got me, Dixie, our friends, and families back home! So what *is* it with you?!" I screeched.

She eyed me in that same weird, frightening manner.

"You can yell at me all you want, but I can say to you now that I'm not backing down from my own resolve. *This* is my new Destiny now and I've accepted it. Why the hell don't *you* accept it as well?!" Man, that was as close to her losing it as I've *ever* seen her.

"Okay, you win, Diamond Flame. You win," I said in resignation to the fact.

I just hope that my own blunt honesty doesn't destroy our friendship…

CHAPTER NINETEEN

Now Dixie, the mentor/teacher of our heroines, takes over:

I didn't believe what I just witnessed in front of my face at that moment. I tell you, if there's one thing I hate more than having the Realm come under attack, it's to see two close friends now practically at each other's throats. That really sickens me to no end!

And, as is my usual practice, I confronted both of them!

"Get over here, you two. NOW!!" I yelled.

That sure got their attention in a flash!!

"What is it, Dixie?" asked Red Ice, playing the innocent act on me.

Pretending to be as cheerful as I usually am, I really let myself loose!!

"Listen up, you two!! I don't know what's *been going on here, but you can bet your last dollar bill that it's going to end right here and* NOW!!*"* Boy, did their eyes just *pop* out of their skulls by then.

After a few milli-seconds went by, they seemed to get the hint -- I hoped.

From the Journals of Diamond Flame:

I had to hand it to Dixie, she didn't take any nonsense or pull her punches when it comes to loyalty. That's her strongest characteristic and when that gets threatened, God, could she really *let loose!!* And for her strong resolve, we thanked her deeply from our hearts.

I turned to Dixie to actually tell her what I just told you.

"Hey, Dixie? We, uh, well, that is to say . . . thank you."

"Thank me for what, may I ask?"

"Well, for getting us back on track and for saving my friendship with Red Ice."

Next it was Red Ice's turn to apologize to Dixie.

"Yeah, Dixie, we don't know what the hell overtook us. It's just that, well, this whole business between Robrack's return and Diamond Flame's new Destiny, well -- frankly, I'm scared half out of my mind!"

"You know something, ladies? There isn't a day that goes by where I'm not feeling even the slightest *twinge of fear for the safety of the Realm. In fact, it* pains *me to have to worry about all*

these Noble Beings that I've entrusted myself to protect. You understand that, don't you?" Her lovely face grew increasingly tortured.

I nodded my head firmly, even as my own face mirrored Dixie's pain.

But you know what they say in regards to fear: it's a mind-killer. And we *did* make a resolve to aid Dixie in protecting the Realm of the Time Beyond Time. There wasn't a chance in hell of anyone stopping us from keeping that promise!!

The time to fight was truly almost upon us!!!

Red Ice, of course, takes up the slack of our adventure:

Boy, I'm glad we got all those dark thoughts out into the open just so we wouldn't have to worry about our feelings compromising our pledge to Dixie. I tell you what, you guys, it really made me all antsy as hell waiting to kick the crap out of Robrack. But I kept running Dixie's command for patience all through my mind.

Soon after that Diamond Flame and I found a little cabin, and settled down for the night, wanting to be as rested as humanly possible. Yet it didn't do much to curb my antsiness.The idea was too exciting!!

As I'm sure Diamond Flame already told you folks, our day would indeed come!!

CHAPTER TWENTY

Red Ice continues where she left off:

When we awoke the following morning, we were greeted not only by the sun (or what passes for one here) but we saw -- yeah, you guessed it. Robrack's airship, still hovering overhead, waiting to make his move...and also waiting for *us* to make *our* move, as well.

Now we felt more than ready, and we got the go-ahead signal from Dixie.

Finally -- *this was IT!!!!*

From the Journals of Diamond Flame:

A new sense of determined resolve flowed all throughout my being as our time drew near. Swiftly I reviewed our battle plan with Red Ice, even though I knew she'd already gotten the idea from the first time we set off to fight.

Only this time...it was going to be for real -- and for *keeps!!*

Dixie, the heroines' mentor/friend tells us more of her thoughts:

A horrible feeling, such as I never had before, consumed me inside my soul. That feeling just happened to be deep regret. Instantly I began to wonder if, in my all-out pledge to keep the Realm safe, that I was putting two innocent lives in severe jeopardy. As I told the girls, and I'm sure you already know by now, however, I can't put my own feelings and concerns ahead of my task. That would constitute a sense of selfishness, and *that's* something I cannot, and just *won't* allow.

All I can now say is that I hope that whatever happens, all turns out alright . . .

Red Ice tells us now of her part in the battle against Robrack:

My excitement grew more and more palpable by the minute. Diamond Flame had by now told me her part, what with her having giant wings and all. *That* much was obvious to all of us. However what *wasn't* so clear was -- what *my* part was in our little plot, as it were.

Somehow, I think Dixie actually sensed that, because without even saying a word, she pointed in the general direction of the Foxtrot Time Works. Already my new strength gave way to my old queasiness, and I wanted to voice this feeling to Dixie. Of course, I dare not . . . at least not at this stage of the game, anyway.

Immediately my mind turned back to the event at hand.

"Hey Dixie, what exactly *is* my part in this plan?" I asked.

Once more she pointed to the Foxtrot Time Works.

"Your job, Red Ice, is to stand on watch and keep an eye out for any of Robrack's troops should they decide to land and march their way to the Time Works. I dare say that's the best I can do for you at this moment."

Sounded like a good plan to me, I thought.

Our old "friend" Robrack interrupts our tale to stick his two cents in:

Well, here I am again, in my new-and-improved airship, which I'm sure you already heard about. No doubt you know by now (maybe by my inadvertantly telling you goody-goodies reading this little escapade) that I planned to take out the Foxtrot Time Works in order to gain my revenge for being defeated. And let me tell you goody-goody readers this much right now: when it comes to a fight or warfare, I'm a really sore loser!!

And what, if anything, can be done to stop me, you ask? Well, if I had my way, not one damn thing! Not one!

Hold on a second! Don't even tell me! Just *don't* even *think* of it!!

From the Journals of Diamond Flame:

I was still formulating my part of the battle plan in my mind; in fact, I was even trying to *perfect* it. I knew what I had to do. The troubling thought I *had* was what I had told Red Ice much earlier as to whether I *was* coming back alive or not.

But as much as I love her, in a big sister way, I had to put that consideration aside on the back burner as I closed my eyes, brought my thoughts into sharp focus, gazed at the sky…and soon found myself airborne, the wind and breeze blowing into my long blond hair.

The feeling was both exhilarating and somber at the same time. My mission -- indeed, my new life's calling -- grew all the more important. I became almost machine-like in my demeanor as I flew my way to Robrack's airship. Even my humor grew silent.

It's now or never, I grimly thought to myself.

CHAPTER TWENTY-ONE

Red Ice lays down the details of her part:

After we returned to the Foxtrot Time Works, our ears were "greeted" by the electronic buzzer

indicating that the shift Mr. Hackett worked was done, and the next bunch could take over. *Oh,*

goody, I sardonically thought to myself.

Presently Mr. Hackett made his way to the exit gate. That's where he saw us…and of course, he

wasn't too happy about it. Not at all in the least bit.

"Oh, it's you two again. What do you want of me *now?!?*" he moaned wearily.

Dixie was the first to answer him.

"Still not going to help out, Mr. Hackett?"

He sighed heavily and angrily.

"Look, I thought I told you ladies that I'm through with all the excitement and adventure. I'd

like to just get home, rest up, and prepare for tomorrow's shift. Besides . . . " he said, "my wife

needs me now more than ever. This whole affair involving our young daughter Skywatcher has

Sunleaf -- that's my wife, in case you had forgotten or didn't know -- emotionally traumatized, and I'm sure she'll agree with my thinking now." I'm not sure but I thought I saw his eyes tear up.

"Look, Mr. Hackett," I told him, "if it'll help I can stand guard at the Time Works till the next shift shows up. That way, if there's any trouble, we can ward it off."

He eyed us skeptically.

"Ha-ha. A likely plan, I say sarcastically. What can *you* do?"

"Oh, you'd be surprised. You'd be *really* surprised."

He still wasn't convinced of that assurance I gave him.

At least, not at first…though *that* would change before too long.

From the Journals of Diamond Flame:

As much as I felt excited about my excursion into natural flight, my mind was still troubled at the increasingly certain prospect of my demise…unless a freaky kind of miracle occurs. Which, in my "normal" mind, was unlikely to happen.

Oh!! Right, I forgot. We're in the Realm of the Time Beyond Time. *Anything* could happen here, so maybe that miracle *wasn't* out of the question, after all.

Swiftly my thoughts returned to the now-stationary airship below my vantage point. I noticed that, like his previous model, it had a laser of some kind; then I remembered that it was the dreaded "octo-laser" I had read a little bit about. But let me say to you that reading about it sure as hell didn't make my task any easier.

Like my young predecessor before me I landed just on the starboard side of the cabin, where the control-panel was located. I had to admit, it was, in spite of the evil it would soon cause, quite *impressive!!*

Entering the cabin, I drew out my long blade, and searched all around the interior. I saw all sorts of dials, keyboards, buttons, and even those new "touch-screens" that seemed to be so common back home.

"Typical of evil ones to arm itself with technology. Just typical," I said out loud to myself, partly to calm my now-itchy nerves.

I was still in the midst of my dazed admiration when a gruff male voice yelled out.

"Hey!! Who the blazes are *you*?!"

I turned around, and found myself face-to-face with Robrack himself -- and I was *shocked as hell!* My jaw dropped!!

"Dr. Brackett??" I whispered even though I knew it wasn't really him.

As far as his fashion statement goes, well, he had on the same clothes he wore when he met his defeat at the hands of young Skywatcher. I couldn't help but laugh at him!

"What's so funny?!" he snarled angrily.

Little did I know that the joke wouldn't be so funny much longer!

CHAPTER TWENTY-TWO

Now Dixie relates more of her observations:

That bad feeling returned with a vengeance greater than Robrack's own and let me say to you now that, of course, it almost sickened me to no end!! It was as if I had done something truly monstrous!!

Against my deepest beliefs and morals I had put two innocent young women's lives in grave danger . . . all out of my now-misguided attempts to keep the Realm from danger!

But I had to hand it to Diamond Flame and Red Ice: they handled it with the utmost confidence and assurance of their own inner strengths. Not to mention their adaptability in the usage of the instructions that I had given them throughout all of these moments in the grand scheme of things, such as they were.

So...maybe this *wouldn't* be the worst thing to happen, after all. In fact, it might turn out for the best...that is, if my two star pupils don't fail themselves or us!!

Then again, as I just told you now, I have the utmost *supreme* confidence.

And *that's* what's going to save the day for us all!

From the Journals of Diamond Flame:

Robrack's hazel eyes narrowed in contemplation as he scanned me up and down, focusing on the wings that had grown out of my shoulders, and gave me the power that I never even *conceived* of having in my "old" life.

"So!! Another of those bird-brained Amazon goody-goodies, I see," he crassly uttered out loud to my face even as I tried not to laugh at his mental density.

"Excuse me, but I detest being called a 'bird-brained Amazon.' I am a Startian, sworn to help keep the Realm safe from power-hungry, anger-driven, badly-dressed twits like *you!!* My name is Diamond Flame, in case you wanted to show at least a *smattering* of good manners," I said, admonishing him along the way.

He shrugged his shoulders as if to say, "Who cares? Not I."

"Now that we know each other," he said to me, "what are you *doing* here?!"

Then my own eyes narrowed in anger.

"Oh, it's simple. You need to be destroyed, along with your mad scheme for the Realm's destruction. And my 'friend,' there's no way in hell that you're going to stop us from fulfilling that vow."

Again he shrugged his shoulders, then he grew confused.

"Who else is in on this altruistic plot?" he asked.

I smiled slightly yet grimly.

"Oh, you'll meet my friend soon enough, and let me warn you now that she does *not* like

tyranny and evil one iota. So if you try anything, she'll kick your ass from here to next

week -- and I do mean that *literally!!*" I hoped he got the message, though logically I knew that

he clearly wouldn't.

Then again, I was glad of that, because soon he'd find out that I don't make idle threats where

lives are concerned. I mean, I didn't accept it as a paramedic, and I sure as hell won't accept it

now!!

Now my patient demeanor, as taught by Dixie, was going out the window.

I wanted to destroy this son-of-a-bitch *now!!!*

Red Ice describes her time at the Foxtrot Time Works:

I spent a hell of a lot time just looking between Robrack's airship and the main building of the Foxtrot Time Works, still waiting for the enemy to make the move -- so I can be ready to kick some major ass!!

Once again I got that stern gaze from Dixie that told me to be patient and wait this out. By then, well, my patience was running out faster than the hourglass sands on *Days of Our Lives* (even though I couldn't stand that show). Also, I think Mr. Hackett's nerves grew more and more raw as the moments dragged on and on, although I'm sure he'd never admit it.

Then, finally, we all turned our sights to the skies . . . and boy, did we get one *hell* of a surprise coming out of the airship!!

Dixie's face grew even more somber than before.

"So -- it's come at last," was all she said at that point.

CHAPTER TWENTY-THREE

From the Journals of Diamond Flame:

A sudden jolt rocked the airship, causing us to momentarily panic -- well, causing *me* to panic, anyway.

"What the hell's *that??!!*" I yelled.

Robrack just stood there laughing his head off.

"Well, my little buxomy blond bird-brained goody-goody, that's *my* little surprise. You see, since the last time I was here, I managed to upgrade my weaponry. See, my new-and-improved octo-laser can now fire on its target autonomously. That jolt you felt was the first blast of said new octo-laser firing down right smack near *the Foxtrot Time Works!!!*"

God, his laugh would make even the most rottem pumpkin throw up!

Swiftly I totally lost my temper by that point. Grabbing him by the back of his coat I whirled him to face me . . . and then proceeded to deck him over and over.

By the time I finished my explosive physical tirade, I was left worn out. Breaking off to catch my breath, I soon found myself looking down the barrel of his laser-pistol which, I'm sure he'd smugly say to me, was also new-and-improved. He was smiling at me, in spite of the beating that I'd given him moments before.

It looked like my suicidal prophecy would soon come to pass…

Red Ice tells us now what she'd *just experienced:*

"Dixie?" I found myself asking, even as I slowly looked back up to the skies -- and my jaw really dropped!!

We'd seen a powerful laser beam shoot downwards from Robrack's airship, hitting a space just inches from the Foxtrot Time Works. God, that was *close!!*

I don't about you, but this was the one time I wish I had Diamond Flame's power of flight. That reminded me -- how is she making out up there?? And is she alright?!

I didn't get any answers to those questions, because another barrage of laser-fire came even closer to the Time Works. Panic was spreading like a California wildfire that's gone out of control!! And there was not one damn thing we could do at this stage.

Unless -- that's *right! Of course!!* I'd totally forgotten all about it!!

"Dixie!! Dixie!!" I shouted out as loud as I could.

Immediately she came running to me.

"What is it, Red Ice?"

My face brightened up exponentially as I began to speak.

"Watch this, Dixie." And with that said, I drew out my blade, pointed it at a nearby boulder, and lifted up the blade slowly as instructed. I moved the blade, with the boulder, toward the airship, and then I swung down as hard as I could!

"Red Ice, NO!!!" screamed Dixie in sudden panic.

Ignoring her, I watched the boulder make its way to Robrack's airship -- only to have its shatter into a billion powdery fragments. I didn't believe it!! I really *didn't!!* The damn thing didn't even hit Robrack's airship at all!!!!

That's when Dixie ran to me, a look of anger on her face.

"You young fool, why did you try *that?! Didn't you realize that his airship can generate a force-field around itself?!?"*

Boy, was I sheepish by then. Ah well, just try and try again.

From the Journals of Diamond Flame:

I sensed in the recesses of my mind what Red Ice attempted, and while it was a good plan, unfortunately it just didn't work against this type of advanced technology. There had to be a more subtle weakness in here somewhere. The trouble was: would it actually work? I had no doubt in my psyche that it would work. All I had to do was to basically look for a needle in a haystack.

Frantically I tried to recall what Skywatcher did to defeat this lunatic the last time around. But I couldn't very well do that with Robrack watching me at every turn, his laser-pistol still fixed on my person.

"Don't even try to look for escape, my bird-brained beauty. There's no way out for you," he smugly said to my face, having fully recovered from the pounding I delivered a long while ago. Yet oddly enough, I didn't become emotionally flustered. In fact, my new resolve allowed me to draw into my own "resting realm."

Closing my eyes I retreated to my realm, all the while trying to formulate a new plan to ensure Robrack's defeat and destruction…and it also allowed me to focus on Red Ice, whom I wished had more success than I.

At this moment, though, that was the *least* of my troubles.

CHAPTER TWENTY-FOUR

Now Dixie tells us some more of her thoughts and feelings:

I wasn't too thrilled with Red Ice's rash decision to attempt to take out Robrack's airship.

Evidently if not obviously she'd forgotten about the automatic force-field that, unfortunately for

us, Hyradian vessels can generate for protection against everything from thrown objects, as in the

case of her boulder, to laser fire.

As is my usual thing of habit, I really let her have it.

"All right, you, what the hell possessed you to try *that* little stunt of yours?!?!"

Sheepishly, Red Ice turned her gaze to me.

"Well, it *was* a thought, and well, I figured I could at least give it a try. Hey, can you blame me

for that ?" she meekly replied, still showing that sheepishly weak smile.

"Well…" I sighed, "all right. This time."

Somehow or other, I could never stay mad at anybody unless I feel that it's really warranted.

And the only person to fit *that* bill is, of course, our old enemy Robrack. So I guess you could

say that Red Ice's intents were good if slightly mis-executed in practice. (I never told anybody this, but in reality I see a lot of myself whenever I look at Red Ice. I mean, I was as impulsive as

she is. Maybe more.)

I only hope that Red Ice's impatience doesn't spell disaster for the Realm . . . and especially for

her and Diamond Flame!!

Once more, our old " friend" Robrack sticks more of his two cents in:

I just couldn't believe what this blond goody-goody bird-woman was doing. Imagine the nerve

of her!! Falling asleep while I'm about to achieve the greatest triumph of my life: the fulfillment

of my ultimate revenge! And she calls herself a *warrior*. Bah!!

Although it *did* arouse a weird curiosity in my mind as to what she's thinking. But trying to

figure out these heroes' motives was one, if not the biggest, weakness I have.

Then again, why on Earth am I telling *you* people all of this?? Can *somebody* answer that?

From the Journals of Diamond Flame:

My stay in my "resting realm" almost drew to a close as my senses became more acute with each

passing second. And I *still* didn't have any plan of action, nor could I recall how Skywatcher did

her feat of heroism. In fact, if anything my "resting realm" offer me *nothing!!*

Suddenly -- I *remembered!!*

Of course!! That's it!! Why the hell didn't I think of if before?

Oh, wait a minute . . . yeah, that's right. Robrack, naturally.

Then . . . hey, yeah!! Right! Sure! *Now* I've got the plan!!

Okay, Mr. Robrack. Now we play the game by *my* rules!!

I can just hope that Red Ice gets the hint sooner or later…

Red Ice graciously concedes this part of the story to another old friend:

Hello again. It's me, Mr. Steve Hackett, back again to relate more of my weird adventures,

unwanted as they are. In a sense, seeing the one called Diamond Flame reminded me, in a sad

way, of my now-long-departed daughter Skywatcher, whom I missed terribly.

Anyway, I stood outside the main gates of the Foxtrot Time Works, ostensibly to make my way

home to see my wife Sunleaf. I'm sure you're already aware this entire experience had

traumatized Sunleaf to almost no end. I mean, how would *you* feel if your only child went on a

great adventure, only to never return home again?

Oh, that's right. Most of you read this J.R.R. Tolkien fellow, huh? I'm sure, however, that Mr.

Tolkien, in all fairness, never prepared anybody to actually *feel* those things on a personal level.

I'm sorry, I don't mean to ramble on and on like this but that loss is still fresh with my wife and I, so do try to forgive me on that.

Where was I? Hmmmm . . . oh, that's right. Our story.

Well, as logically as I can tell, my new companions gazed at the skies above our heads. What they waited for, I couldn't dare to guess, though I *did* remember that it had to do with *Robrack!!* If there's one name I never wish to hear again, that's it!! What an appalling "man" he was and if I, for one, ever look upon his face once more -- well, what I'd do would surely get me arrested!!

Anyway . . .getting back to my part in this little rehash of my unwanted adventure, I stood with the young red-haired woman called Red Ice, just idly chatting about partly out of good manners but mostly to calm my own shaky nerves in spite of the fact that I *still* had to get home to mywife Sunleaf who, as I stated many a time earlier, was distraught over the loss of Skywatcher.

Then, oddly enough, a slight smile drew itself across my face. I turned my gaze to Red Ice and her elder companion, the woman named Dixie. I'm not sure what made me think this, but it seems to me that my confidence in these two -- check that; make it *three* brave women

(I had forgotten about the one called Diamond Flame, up there in the skies of the Realm).

Maybe, just maybe…this might turn out for the best after all, I thought.

Now Red Ice goes back to telling her side of the story…as usual by now:

Hey thanks, you guys, for letting Mr. Hackett do his thing in telling his thoughts of these events that somehow sashayed their way, unwanted, into his life. Sure could've used the break, I tell you. It even gave me the chance to further my own strategy in the hopes of defeating Robrack once and for all Time, if you'll pardon that crass remark given our locale.

Then, immediately my thoughts unexpectedly turned back to Diamond Flame, who was still up on that hideous airship, suffering a God-knows-what kind of trouble . . .

CHAPTER TWENTY-FIVE

From the Journals of Diamond Flame:

My sudden clarity gave way to a slight uncertainty even as I kept my hard resolve in mind as I continued to struggle to evade Robrack's sickeningly ever-present watch over my person. Emotionally and psychologically I felt as if I was being-- *violated!!* That feeling nauseated me to no end!!

Then my clarity returned with a sudden jolt of inspiration. All I needed now was a distraction, as I'm sure I told you earlier. Sure!!

Figuring I had nothing left to lose, I drew out my long blade (I forgot all about it during the course of everything) and flashed it in Robrack's face, smiling confidently.

Naturally, he didn't like *that* at all.

"What are you trying to do, as if I had to ask?" he queried.

I didn't dignify that with a response, at least not a *verbal* one. For you see, I remembered Dixie's instructions on my sword-play. In other words -- *batter up!!*

Robrack's eyes just about damn near *popped* out of their sockets as I swung my blade in the manner Dixie taught me, and then -- the most *delightful* thing occurred.

And what *was* that thing, you ask of me?

Well, it wasn't the most *effective* thing, I admit, but what happened was a small but obviously vital piece of machinery ruptured from the control-panel, sending sparks flying all around us. Now, I know that Dixie said not to use the sword to kill anyone…but she *didn't* say anything about enemy *machines* now, did she?

Unbelievably, as is usually the case anymore, Robrack laughed uproariously.

And why is *that?*

See, unbeknownst to me Robrack's airship was now featuring an automatic repair system wherein any piece of the vessel was fixed by group of micro-bots!!

Damn!! Why the hell *are* these villains always up on the latest technology?!

Then not surprisingly, Robrack gloated as if he was a kid at Christmastime.

"Well, well, well, my busty bird-backed goody-goody. Thought you had the upper hand on me, huh? Well, you thought wrong now, didn't you?!? *This* time it's me, the scourge of the Realm, who has the hand now!!" he boomed, even now drawing his laser-pistol out of his holster . . . and aiming it at my head.

For the first time, I felt the deathily icy grip of fear on my body . . .

Dixie, the girls' mentor/closest friend, tells us more of her sense of things:

I felt a sudden chill race down my back, as if a cold burst came from out of nowhere (and that's in the *literal* sense of it all, of course). Then my forehead dripped with a frosty sweat -- and somehow I *knew!!*

Red Ice took notice of this right away.

"Hey, Dixie? You okay? What's wrong?"

I don't know why I told her, but she *had* to know.

"I can sense…panic. Fear. Worry. And…it's coming from *up there!!*" I pointed to the sky—and Robrack's airship!!

Red Ice's eyes grew wide in shock!

"You don't mean -- ?!"

I nodded coldly. "Yep. I can feel it from *Diamond Flame!!*"

"Oh wow!! We've got to help her, Dixie!!"

Somberly I agreed. Only I couldn't figure out how...

CHAPTER TWENTY-SIX

From the Journals of Diamond Flame:

A cold sweat permeated my brow as my eyes continually stared out at the laser-pistol still

pointed at my head. Rapidly my steely resolve melted into an all-out dose of terror . . . and I was

ready to lose it. Well, almost.

All of a sudden, I received a hunch. No, not a hunch. A message, and it was coming from below

the ship. In fact, I believed it came from . . . *all right!! Now I get it!!*

My terror drifted away, and my steel resolve was re-forged stronger than ever.

Of course, I'll bet you're wondering what I'm talking about here, right?

Well, that's my little secret, and I really can't divulge it at this time. Sorry, but suffice it to say

that it woke me up exponentially.

And thus, with a good Batgirl-style karate kick I knocked the laser-pistol out of Robrack's

disgustingly manicured hand, and before he recovered his wits I kicked it again -- this time out of

the cabin, letting it plummet to the ground below.

So it went for the third time, only now I kicked him in his stomach. He doubled over in pain and anger. Naturally, as is my thing, of course, I just laughed at his misery.

"You airhead bimbo!! Now you're *really* going to get!!" he roared in rage. Speedily he ran up to me, his hands reaching for my throat. Sidestepping his rather pathetic maneuver I returned with a good upper-cut, like my dad showed me from the boxing on TV.

I wanted more of *this* sort of action!! But the mission's importance grew ever-so-increasingly prevalent.

I re-drew my blade, ready for another attempt at some feminine-style sabotage when I heard that gruff, crassly familiar voice shout out.

"Don't even *think* of trying *that* little stunt again!!"

I whirled, and saw that Robrack had drawn out a blade of his own. And I had to hand it to him, he looked like he was adept at swordplay himself.

Like the last time around, he was in for one *hell* of a rude awakening!!

Red Ice relates how she prepared for her showdown:

The three of us, namely Dixie, Mr. Hackett, and myself, witnessed the enemy airship inch itself

closer and closer to the main body of the Foxtrot Time Works, ready to lay it to total waste and

ruin, and with it the entire Realm of the Time Beyond Time as well.

Mr. Hackett then developed a weird twinkle in his eyes.

"You know, ladies, you've just convince me to change my mind after all. I can only hope that my

wife Sunleaf understands all of this. It wasn't easy the last time about and well, I don't want my

marriage wrecked."

"Don't worry about Sunleaf, Steve. We'll take care of that," said Dixie.

"WE?!" I gasped in shock.

Without saying anything more to me, Dixie requested Mr. Hackett's address and having gotten it,

she and I made our way to his home and his wife. Man, I couldn't believe my senses by then!! I

mean, has Dixie flipped her wig, or what?

In her usual manner, she turned to me.

"I know what you're thinking, Red Ice. And I can assure you now this is all part of the mission."

Knowing better than to argue, I didn't say one thing . . . but that *didn't* keep me from *wondering* about that little plan. But…Dixie knew best, so I went along with it.

Man alive, I wished I was in Diamond Flame's shoes right now . . .

From the Journals of Diamond Flame:

I don't know about you, but this was definitely the *one* time I wish I had Red Ice up here with me. Then we'd *really* give this chauvanistic throwback a run for his money. But I figured she's already got her hands full guarding the Foxtrot Time Works from the next vile installment in his insane plot for personal revenge! All that because he wouldn't take his lumps like a man. Now *that's* typical of some men, I suppose.

But this *wasn't* the time for any more philosophical musings. I had a villain to defeat -- and I had to defeat him *now!!*

CHAPTER TWENTY-SEVEN

Now our land-bound trio sets off on a slight detour, as described by Red Ice:

Well, here we are, folks. The modest home of Mr. and Mrs. Steve Hackett. I mean, that's what it said on the mailbox, right?

Anyway, we three casually strolled into the house, with Mr. Hackett leading the way. After all, it's *his* house . . . well, his and his wife's, all things being allegedly equal in marriages. At least, that's what I've *heard.*

The moment we stepped in, Mr. Hackett called out as loud as he reasonably could.

"Sunleaf, we're home."

Instantly a youngish woman literally *flew* into the living room (that's where we were), landing almost directly on his toes. She was somewhat tall, with long black hair ending in close-cut bangs, had dusky, brownish skin, and large wings growing out of her shoulders. Her clothes were a heavy-knit floral-designed blouse, form-fitting blue jeans, and black pump shoes.

She smiled at first, then grew ever-so-slightly unhappy.

"Uh, Steve, you didn't tell me we were having company," she said.

"Oh, well, to be honest, I didn't know myself till a while ago," he replied.

Then good old Dixie loudly cleared her throat.

"Oh, Sunleaf, I'd like you to meet Red Ice," he told her, first pointing to me along the way, and then to Dixie, "and this is Dixie."

"Hello, Red Ice. Dixie," greeted Sunleaf, looking at us. "Now, Steve . . . " continued Sunleaf, turning back to her husband, "what the hell are they *doing* here?!?!"

Before Steve -- let's skip this formal palabra-dabra-ba -- could answer, Dixie calmly intervened on his behalf, not to mention ours as well.

"Mrs. Hackett -- I mean, Sunleaf -- I just informed your husband, and I think it's only right for me to tell you that your old enemy Robrack has escape his imprisonment, and even as we speak now, has already made his way to the Foxtrot Time Works."

Sunleaf eyed us as if we were a bowl of rancid pasta salad.

"And what the hell does this have to do with *us*?!? As if I had to ask," she said in an obviously angry manner, mixed with a little piece of sadness.

I just stared out, not knowing what to say to her. Of course, Dixie *did* know what to say.

"Look, Sunleaf, believe me when I tell you that I fully understand the loss of your daughter to whatever Destiny the Fates of Time had in store for her. I know you're going through a trying time now, but we need your help as well as your husband's in keeping the Realm safe and getting rid of Robrack once and for all!*"*

For a few minutes Sunleaf stood there speechless, and then the tears rolled down her lovely young face. Her pain and loss were bluntly obvious, and that pain registered on Steve's face as well. In fact, I suspect this is one loss they'll *never* recover from . . . unless some weird thing or other happens. And in this Realm -- well, you get the idea, I'm sure.

"All right . . . when do we start?" asked Sunleaf in resignation.

Dixie and I just looked at each other. We nodded our heads.

"Right away!!" boomed Dixie.

Soon we set off -- and I was *definitely* ready to kick Robrack's sorry ass now!!

CHAPTER TWENTY-EIGHT

We returned to the Foxtrot Time Works, which still stood firm and strong. Hooray for us, I say with mild sarcasm. Hooray.

Within seconds our collective gaze glanced upward and there, lo and behold, the enemy airship had now advanced even closer to the section where the main machines were housed. My teeth grinded so hard they felt ready to crack!!

Soon the Hacketts looked at each other. Now they *really* wanted to aid us, not only for their friends and neighbors whose lives were endangered, but also to honor their daughter who, I suspect, would want them to help us, anyway.

All they needed now a plan of some sort!!

From the Journals of Diamond Flame:

The engine nacelles of the airship whined down, and we found ourselves in stationary position directly above the main housing console of the Foxtrot Time Works. Robrack, being Robrack, was just full of himself. As I told you people over and over, that's typical.

Having just looked out of the portal window at the building down below, he turned his smugly unctuous gaze to my eyes.

"Well, my little busty goody-goody airborne Amazon, feast your peepers on *this!!*"

Instantly the automatic-programmed octo-laser fired the first barrage on the building, causing a side wall to rupture!! *Oh God, no, no!!* I thought as tears welled up even as a horrible sense of nausea overwhelmed me!!

Then -- *I blew out the fuse of logic!!*

Rapidly I drew out my blade, and grew berserk with rage. Left and right I swung my sword, laying waste to anything that came into contact, including Robrack *himself!!* In my anger I totally ignored Dixie's warnings about the blade not to be used to harm a living Noble Being. My reasoning: Robrack didn't exactly *count* as a Noble Being now, did he?

Franticallly he ran all around the cabin like a headless if not *brainless* chicken as the octo-laser kept up a steady stream of barrage after barrage.

I was out for blood . . . and I wasn't to be denied!!!

Red Ice looks upon pure terror; here she, naturally, tells us about it:

My nauseous fear returned with more than a double dose of vengeance as Robrack's hyperactive airship continued to fire shot after shot, not caring what, or more importantly, *who* it hit!!!

In a few seconds I lowered my head to the ground just so I could throw up! Then my combined fear and nausea gave way in only one milli-second, to a steel-hard resolve mixed in with all the anger I could muster up!!

I gazed long and hard at Dixie, who returned my gaze.

She nodded, thus giving me the go-ahead.

God almighty, was I *ever* waiting for this!!

CHAPTER TWENTY-NINE

Now Sunleaf relates her story, albeit somewhat reluctantly:

Well, here we go again.

It's time for little ol' me, Sunleaf Hackett, to play the same part in yet another nutty, hair-raising if not *hare-brained* adventure. Right now, people, this is just about -- no, no, make it, *definitely* the last thing Steve and I wanted. I mean, my God, we just lost our *daughter!* And an adventure was most emphatically *not* going to cure our emotional distress, believe me.

Anyway…we three, namely Steve, the redhead called Red Ice, and myself, stood just outside the Foxtrot Time Works, waiting for the next barrage of fire from the vile airship above our heads. Quickly I glanced at Steve, taking note of his tightly-clenched jaw. Whenever he did that, usually it means his temper was growing increasingly short. Then again, it *could* mean that he was mad at himself for leaving his favorite weapon, namely his old Gibson Les Paul electric guitar, at home. His quick gaze at me said as much.

Then a sweetly toned female voice called out to us.

"Hello, all." It was the woman called Dixie. She was smiling brightly at us. In fact a little *too* brightly, I thought.

We turned and looked at her. In her arms was . . . *Steve's old guitar!!*

Like a kid at Christmastime, Steve ran like hell and happily grabbed the guitar. I stood there, shaking my head humorously. I couldn't help but feel relieved by this sight, and I knew that he'd definitely need it *now!!*

Red Ice returns to tell us her *plan of attack:*

Well, you guys, all I can say is, "Here we go again." I wanted to try out the move I attempted before. You know, the one that got me chewed out by Dixie. I think I told you about that, didn't I? Yeah, I'm sure I did.

But that's in the Past. Then again, what *isn't* around this place?

Oh, I'm getting off-track here, huh? Well, getting back to my train of thought, I once more pointed my blade at another nearby boulder, taking care not to over-exert myself. Slowly, almost reverently I towed the boulder, aimed it at the airship's aft (that's the back of the ship, in case you guys didn't know), and then struck with all the might I could muster!!

Then . . . oh, *damn!!* Nothing!! Again!!!

However I *did* get the sense that the force-field was actually weakening, although I couldn't at first figure out why but I can bet it had something to do with the octo-laser's power usage . . . but don't quote me on that. After all, it's *only* a guess.

Now a new and not-so-happy thought popped into my head: I wondered how Diamond Flame was faring up there, all by her lonesome . . .

From the Journals of Diamond Flame:

The battle between Mr. Robrack and myself ended in a sort of draw . . . for the time being, anyway. We were both physically worn out, but I felt the tide of the war turning on my favor. At least, that's what I *hoped* for.

Then I gave a quick glance at the control-panel, and noticed a small red light flashing almost indistinctly. My curiosity mounted -- and always at the most inopportune moments, too. Yet I couldn't just put it out of my mind.

I drew into a mist of inattentiveness when I suddenly felt a rush of minute wind whiz past my ears, along with a slight cut on my face . . . and another hideously out-of-tune roar!

Swiftly I resumed my fighting stance…and of course, I decked the hell out of Robrack once more, and some more after that. In fact, I could kept this up all day!

Then . . . *yeah, sure!!!*

With not a second to lose I made my move.

Speedily I flew out of the airship, and landed not more than five feet from the Foxtrot Time Works, where I was met by Red Ice, Dixie, Mr. Hackett, and a young Startian woman that I figured was his wife Sunleaf. You know, Skywatcher's mother.

Red Ice ran up to me, hugging the stuffings out of me.

"You're alive! You're *really* alive!!" she wept out in joy and relief.

I embraced her as tightly as I could, thus echoing that feeling.

"I'm glad to see you, too, Red Ice."

As always, good old Dixie interrupted us in the ever-so-present common sense manner she continually managed to use in these scenarios.

"Sorry about this, Diamond Flame, but we don't have a whole hell of a lot of time for happy reunions, as much as I'm relieved to see you. There's still *the matter of finding a way to defeat Robrack once and for all!!"*

Instantly my face brightened up exponentially!

"Hey Dixie, I just remembered how Skywatcher did it!"

Red Ice's jaw dropped in sudden realization.

"Oh *wow, man!* That's right! I just remembered that myself!" she yelled.

Dixie smiled, while the Hacketts looked at me in shock!

I went up to Mr. Hackett.

"Pardon me, but do you have any -- *dishwashing detergent* in your house?"

He gave me a very incredulous look, as if I had lost my mind. Then his own eyes boggled in
realization, though it wasn't the joyous kind. I should have guessed. The Hacketts still had their
little girl on their minds. That's understandable, considering all the hell they're going through.

I only hope this actually *works!!*

CHAPTER THIRTY

Unfortunately, our old "friend" Robrack has to tell more of his plan:

I, for one, am getting more than a little bit tired of the constant pounding that I've been receiving a lot of lately in the game. Up until now, it's all been fun and jollies, but now it's all-out, no-holds-barred total *destruction!!* And I dare any of you goody-goodies to try and stop me!! Because if you do, you'll be the sorriest sort on the face of this Universe!!

From now on, as the saying goes, it's no more Mr. Nice Guy -- as if I actually was a nice guy, anyway . . .

Red Ice picks up the tale again, as usual:

The race was on to get the dish soap ready to implement Diamond Flame's part of the plan to ensure the total defeat of Robrack.

And maybe you're asking yourself just why the *hell* we needed dishwashing liquid. Well, here's your answer, friend: it was influenced by Skywatcher, in case you'd forgotten . . . which, if you've been following all of this, is highly unlikely.

Finally we reached the Hacketts' house, where immediately Sunleaf -- that's Steve's wife, obviously -- got the jumbo-size bottle from underneath her sink in the kitchen. Then she remembered to grab a bucket of water, having filled it up along the way.

Now the main problem with this was: how are we going to get it to Robrack's airship? I mean, we couldn't just *run* with it.

Oh, that's right, I forgot. There was Dixie, ready for the task.

And so, Dixie spread her arms at great length, allowing us to be teleported back to where we left minutes before. She's really good at that, you know.

Then we got to work, and it had to be fast because, if you'll excuse the remark, Time was the one essence running out on us! And God, was it *ever!!*

From the Journals of Diamond Flame:

"Are you sure this'll work *this* time?!"

That question from Sunleaf Hackett greeted my ears as I prepared to mix the soapy water bucket.
Deep in the recesses of my mind I knew that it *had* to work. The entire Realm was depending on this.

Somehow or other I think I got a sense of *déjà vu* coming from the Hacketts, especially Sunleaf.
In a painfully sad way, it reminded her too much of their young daughter Skywatcher. The next few moments made this all too clear.

When I finshed mixing the soapy water, I turned and walked up to Sunleaf.

"I'm sure it'll work, Sunleaf," I answered, placing a sympathetic hand on her shoulder. She smiled ever so slightly even as the tears rolled down her lovely dark face. Believe me, I understood her grief and sorrow.

But -- and not to be cold or something -- the mission, like Dixie told us numerous times, just *had* to take full precedence over all other matters where the entire Realm's fate was concerned. Sometimes, though, I really wondered at Dixie's supposed "wisdom" on these things of the heart. But I'm not here to judge; that's History's job to do that.

Now, to our momentary relief, Dixie takes over for a bit:
I don't really know what Diamond Flame actually told you, but I can bet she was dead-on accurate in her deductions. Now, you might think that I'm as cold as a leftover cheeseburger in the Hacketts' meat drawer. Well, nothing's more further from the truth on the subject. My biggest problem is that -- well, I care just *maybe* a little too much. But my reasoning is that if I didn't care, I'd let the entire Realm suffer . . . and I wouldn't give one tinker's damn. Fortunately, that just isn't *me* now, is it?!

Now . . . getting back on track here, after Diamond Flame mixed the water and soap, as I'm sure she told you just moments before, she gazed up at the skies above, focusing on Robrack's vile if somewhat impressive airship. I shook my head in utter disgust. All that wondrous technology,

and it had to be used for evil!!

Well . . . if all goes according to plan, *that* little idea would change soon enough!!

CHAPTER THIRTY-ONE

Here we let Mr. Steve Hackett take over:

I didn't understand why, but a new and more daring resolve entered into my still somewhat

brittle mindset. Somehow it's as if I sense a . . . *message* of some sort or other. And it *wasn't*

from Diamond Flame or her companions, or even my wife. No, I felt it was coming from --

Skywatcher!!

Sunleaf turned her gaze to me rather perplexedly.

"Steve? Are you okay?"

I didn't readily answer her, but a faint grin on my face said as much as could be said in this

circumstance.

Slowly it dawned on her that maybe, just *maybe,* things would improve for us.

At least I *hoped* that they improved…

Once more, Red Ice picks up the slack of our adventure:

Boy, I tell you, when the action picks up around here, it *really* picks up! And man, I was getting

really excited abut it, too!

Okay, enough with the elated ranting, on to business.

The bucket of the Hacketts' soapy water was ready to go. We decided to finalize our plan to fully ensure Robrack's defeat if not total destruction. And what is the plan, you ask?

Well, just follow along as best as you can, and you'll get the idea in a nutshell. Not unlike Robrack, I say somewhat appropriately in this case.

To start off, Dixie waltzed up to Diamond Flame and Steve.

"Okay, Diamond Flame. You know what to do in regards to your part, am I correct on this?" she asked of Diamond Flame.

"Got it, Dixie," replied Diamond Flame.

Nodding her head, she turned then to Steve. Right away he got his part of the plan confirmed, and if I read the story right the first time, it had something to do with his guitar. Oh, right. I forgot about *that*. I just remembered that Robrack absolutely *detests* rock music. The look on Steve's face said that fact clearly.

Finally she walked to me, eyeing me intently.

"Now, Red Ice. Are you ready for the final round?"

I made no hesitation in answering that question.

"You damn well bet I am, Dixie!! I'm *more* than ready now!!"

The battle -- no, the *war* had finally begun!!

And *this* time . . . it *really* was for keeps!!

Winner takes it all!!!

CHAPTER THIRTY-TWO

From the Journals of Diamond Flame:

The plan went down without a single hitch. Here's how it went: Dixie sent me back up to Robrack's airship, ostensibly to distract him. Then afterwards she teleported Mr. Hackett, armed with the soapy water bucket, and -- I thought this strange at first glance -- his electric guitar. As I said just now, I didn't get the connection…until I suddenly remembered that Robrack emphatically did *not* like rock music. Of course! That's what Moon Swan, in the story, told Mr. Hackett.

In a quick passing of time, I found myself back in the airship's control-cabin. Oddly enough, there wasn't one sign of Robrack anywhere. I imagined, rightfully if not logically, that he might have gone to the restroom to, uh -- *relieve* himself.

Little did he know that his relief was not to last that much longer!

Now Dixie, the duo's friend and mentor, takes over:

A new feeling of relieved joy overcame me as I teleported Mr. Hackett, with water bucket and guitar in hands, up to the airship mere moments after Diamond Flame took to the skies ahead of him. Now, I'm not sure but I thought I saw a mixed glimmer of resolve and anger combined. Maybe it was all in my imagination. Then again . . . maybe *not.*

Well, anyway, here's hoping this works the second time around...

Red Ice once more relates her part of the plan:

As soon as Diamond Flame and Steve made their way back to Robrack's blimp of doom, Dixie turned and looked at me in the most intense manner imaginable.

"Okay, Red Ice, now we're going to try this again. And this time I'm sure as hell certain that it'll work. If it doesn't -- well, let's not think about that, huh?!" I thought I saw her eyes grow beet-red, but maybe that was just me.

Anyway, she had me wait with patience, which is definitely *not* my strongest attribute, I freely admit. With all the effort I could muster, I did so.

"Hey, Dixie, what's gonna happen next?" I asked.

"Just keep watching, Red Ice," Dixie told me, her own patience swiftly running out on her . . . which, I suppose is, only natural, in this case. I mean, wouldn't *your* patience run out if *you* were in our shoes?

Wordlessly from that moment onwards, I kept watch, waiting for the proverbial other shoe to drop, as they say.

Only I didn't know that it would ultimately be taken *literally!!*

From the Journals of Diamond Flame:

Mr. Hackett and I stood in the control-cabin, tensely glancing around, trying to hear for any sign of our insidious foe. I remained calm and tranquil, whereas Mr. Hackett was sweating out buckets as his jaw increasingly tightened. He gripped his guitar like a vise.

At that moment we heard the unmistakable sound of a toilet flush. In spite of the tense moment, we allowed ourselves a good laugh.

Why were we laughing, you ask?

Well, that sound reminded me of the Universe's lovable bigoted grouch, namely the renowned Archie Bunker, of 704 Hauser St., Queens, NY.

Just as sudden as the laughter occurred, it quickly died down . . . because that was when Robrack himself showed up. As always is the case anymore, he didn't look too happy to see me.

"Well, well. My 'favorite' busty bird-brained goody-goody heroine is back, I see," he calmly said in his oily sarcastic way. Then upon seeing Mr. Hackett his cool manner instantly evaporated, giving way to an uncontrollable rage!!

"YOU!! YOU!!" he roared out hoarsely.

Immediately he flew up to Mr. Hackett, fists ready to strike at this innocent husband and father. Mr. Hackett side-stepped out of Robrack's range and thwacked him with the guitar, sending the foe down to the floor.

Robrack turned and glared at my teammate.

"So!! The old electric guitar thing again, huh?? What's your plan now, Hackett? A little ditty about Cleopatra's Needle?! Or a cha-cha dance tune??!!"

Wordlessly Mr. Hackett calmly walked to the main control panel, a strange look on his young face.

Robrack and I looked at each other in total confusion, not sure what to expect.

Mr. Hackett raised the guitar as high as it could go, and soon swung down with all the righteously angry strength he could summon.

The blows were perfectly on target, as pieces of machinery found themselves airborne all around the room…

"Diamond Flame!! The water bucket!! *Now!!!*" shouted my teammate.

All Time froze in place as I lifted the bucket.

"Oh, no. Not again," uttered Robrack in weary sad resignation.

I threw the water at the gaps in the control panel.

Then…*cataclysm!!!*

CHAPTER THIRTY-THREE

Once more, Red Ice takes up the slack of the adventure:

I can't even begin to describe the awe I felt as the first set of explosions from the airship reached our eyes. But that feeling *was* somewhat mixed with a good dose of fear and regret as thoughts of Diamond Flame and Steve popped into our heads. It was especially hard on Sunleaf, I know.

Then it was *my* turn!!

"Red Ice!! Now!!" commanded Dixie.

Instantly I repeated the trick I tried twice before, which was to aim my blade at a nearby boulder and swing down on the ship. *This* time it definitely worked, because the ship's aft side suddenly caved in. Then, repeating the same trick, I sashayed my way to right stern, where the octo-laser was located. *Paydirt!!*

Then, much to our shock Sunleaf took off to the skies! Just like *that!!*

Now Sunleaf relates her plan to aid her husband:

Like the last time I did this little trick, I made my way to the exploding cabin of the airship, trying to help my husband escape. But how?

Fortunately the smoke cleared out enough where he was able to see me.

"Sunleaf!! Oh, not again," he jokingly moaned, clearly relieved to see me.

Swiftly I grabbed him, all the while looking at his shattered guitar. The one called Diamond Flame had snatched Robrack by the back of his neck!

Then we *fled like hell!!!*

Dixie, the mentor/friend of our daring damsel duo, ends the tale:

After Robrack's airship was destroyed and all aboard safe on land, I took Robrack off Diamond Flame's hands, and with all my rage, gave him the physical shellacking he so rightfully deserved. Then I summoned the Fates of Time, of whom I'm one, and bade them to exile this filth to whatever imprisonment was deemed necessary. I only hope that *this* time he won't even dare *think* of escape.

As for the Hacketts, well, we thanked them for their assistance and help in keeping the Realm safe and tranquil. I know it wasn't easy for them, but they handled it magnificently in spite of it all.

Now, I'll bet you're wondering about the Destinies of Diamond Flame and Red Ice, aren't you?

Well…let's just say that their new Destiny has only just begun.

And what about their next part of the tale, you ask?

Since I'm one of the Fates of Time . . . I already know the outcome.

And *that's* something I won't reveal.

At least, not yet, anyway….

And thus ends the First Book

in the Chronicles of Diamond Flame and Red Ice.

AUTHOR'S AFTERWORD

A lot of considerable work and a great deal of thought went into this part of the Annals of the Time Beyond Time, which I'm proud to have conceived. For that, I'd like to thank the following whose influences cannot be discounted: Fritz Leiber, Robert E. Howard, J.R.R. Tolkien, Michael Moorcock, Terry Brooks, Stephen R. Donaldson, Anne McCaffrey, Jules Verne, and Edgar Rice Burroughs.

I'd also like to dedicate this particular tale to the memory of:

JULIE LONDON

1924-2000

And to all those whose love is of SF and fantasy, this one's for you.

Sincerely yours,

Thomas R. Skidmore,

Western Pennsylvania,

November 10, 2010

This edtion is a revised and expanded version of the original December 2010 text. Punctuation and formating reflect these changes.

There are worlds and times beyond our own, yet the problems all the Noble Beings encounter are as comparable as ours. Chief amongst these is the idea of a "system" of rules and regulations called "laws", ostensibly designed to keep overall Harmony and maintenance of the Temporal Balance.

Also amongst them is another "idea", this one allegedly related to the notion of a "Bureaucracy" made to service Mankind's various dilemmas, such as employment, housing, and others needed to provide "security"...but not Hope.

But what if those notions proved themselves to be a lie? How would the Noble Beings react to such dark, grim truths revealed to them? And what would the results be for the Temporal Balance?

This, then, is the result of such a notion, being the tale of one man's lone fight against these false "altruisms . . ."

CHAPTER ONE

"You have been found guilty of the charge against you. Now accept your sentence."

That's precisely how this grand adventure started for me.

And what *was* that charge of which I was convicted?

Well . . . *that's* a rather long story, so the best thing I can do is to just carry on with it as logically

as I can. I'll let the minute details tend for themselves as they see fit, thank you very much.

Now...on with it, I say with little aplomb.

And, as I stated just now, it began with my sentencing:

"Now, FGTR-5183, since you have *been found guilty, you are hereafter confined to spend your*

now eternal days adrift in the Flows of the Oceans of Time and Space, never to return to you former life. You can observe, but never interact with anyone so shall long as your existence endures. Now . . . have you anything to say before the sentence commences?"

"Yes, just this," I said to my unseen accusers, even now hidden within the dark shadows of their advanced machinery. "Your so-called 'charges' are nothing more than a weak attempt to make yourselves look all pious and altruistic in the eyes of all the Noble Beings. But you can't fool *them!*" I smiled at my new-found courage.

"So noted. Let the sentence commence."

And in the quickest instant of Time I found myself suddenly encased in a crystallised gem-like pod-ship, now lifting itself off the ground and thrusting itself, and me, into the Vast Oceans of Limitless Space and Time, never to age, never to interact; only to observe…and think.

Thus my little sojourn into basic Infinity began. I had to admit to myself that the prospect wasn't all that daunting and traumatic for me in the slightest bit. (Now I know what the Kryptonian criminals felt in *Superman: The Movie.)* But, for the sake of repeating myself for those who have a rather short attention span, I didn't feel any fear or worry at all.

In fact, in a very odd and weird manner I actually *welcomed* this!!

CHAPTER TWO

The moment I left my now-former home world behind for all Known Eternity, a strange, dreamy sense of . . . I don't know-- *triumph* coursed itself througout my entire essential being. My accusers knew I'd found them out, and they were definitely quite unready to face the truth about themselves, and as a result, they'd held that damnable so-called "trial" just to eliminate the one lone threat to their plans of subversive conquest of the Realm...namely, myself. The bloke who even now is relating all this to those who have a sense of True Justice, regardless of the "laws".

With all the (if you'll pardon the expression) Time in the Universe to myself, I contemplated all the Myriad Worlds now moving about their various orbits below my vantage point. I have to say to you now I was truly *fascinated* by it all!! I mean, just imagine, if you can, all the Known and Unknown Worlds, unaware that even now they're being watched, nor caring if they *were* aware.

It's as if I felt -- oh, what's the word? -- *omnipotent,* that's it. Sure. I mean, it felt *great!!*

But...those feelings swiftly, and without warning, fell by the waysides of my mind as the full realization of the Judges' sentence fully sunk into my consciousness. As I said, though, then again, it was a sort of -- I don't know -- *escape* from the drudgery of it all.

Oh…you're still wondering about my actual crime, are you not?

Well…as I said, it *is* a rather long story, and all I ask for now is that you allow me this minute luxury of relating it in my own fashion. No need to rush this now, is there?

Getting back onto my original train of thought, I continued to stare endlessly at the Myriad Worlds of the area I now knew was the Time Beyond Time, where warfare and all other various states of dilemmas were virtually if not totally nonexistent, as it were, though how it got to that stage I couldn't even dare try to guess. Indeed, I couldn't even try to guess how I actually *knew* about the Time Beyond Time. That was supposed to be a Universe unto itself, only rarely coming into contact with other Universes, mine included, naturally.

Fortunately I had read accounts -- well, *stories,* really, though I imagined, at the time, that they were nothing more than flights of some writer's imagination. I have to say that for once (at least in this case) I was *pleased* to be wrong.

I was still in the midst of my daydreaming -- well, *time*-dreaming when there came upon me a sudden, violent jolt of energy force, sending me whirling about and around. I don't know about you, but let me be the first to say that it definitely *wasn't* a pleasant experience, believe me on that, friends.

Anyway, I then found myself hurtling toward a nearby planetoid just below my vantage point…

and I was descending *fast!!!* The calm resolve that I maintained throughout gave way to a

nausea-inducing panic!! It was all I could do to keep from screaming. I mean, who'd actually

hear me, anyhow??

I thought to myself I *wouldn't* remain alive long enough to relate *this* experience…

CHAPTER THREE

The minute I entered the planetoid's orbital field, I began thinking that maybe, just *maybe*, I'd survive after all. In the back of my mind, however, there still lingered the remnants of doubt in that bit of logic. But then again, *true* logic, such as it is, was never my one strong suit.

Then, unbelievably enough, my rate of descent actually *slowed* almost to the proverbial snail's pace, as it were. Thus with the softest landing imaginable, I found myself safe and somewhat sound on solid land.

There was still the matter of my crystal pod-ship. How the hell was I to get out of it?

In another inexplicable moment, the answer to *that* question came in the fact that now the crystal pod-ship was gradually turning itself into a soft powder sprinkling itself all about me. I felt my eyeballs boggle in confused delight.

"Thank you." I said to the now-granulated remains, a slight grin on my face.

Shaking off the leftover powder, I thus began a rather quick glance around my landing position. A new sense of freedom, as I'd never felt even *before* my "trial", ran throughout my being. *This was GREAT!!* I thought to myself.

Then a totally *new* thought wormed its way into my mind.

"Where is everybody?" I asked myself aloud.

Realizing that an answer would definitely *not* come my way anytime soon, I began my search in a rather haughty-like if not all-out earnest manner. I hadn't known this upon landing, but it grew blatantly obvious that it was *hot as hell!!!* In a very sarcastic manner I "thanked" the Judges for this little sojourn onto a desert planetoid, with no cold liquid refreshment of any sort, nor any sort of settlement or civilization what-so-ever.

Soon my new-found freedom momentarily gave way to a minute despair as my search for *any* sign of friendly life dragged on and on. And my body temperature increased exponentially as did my blood pressure…and a feeling of dizziness now overwhelmed me.

Then, just as I was more than ready to collapse from total exhaustion, a young voice, evidently of the female persuasion, called out loudly in my direction.

"Hello?! Is anyone out here?!"

Swiftly I called out.

"Over here!!"

And *that*, I dare say to you, was the last thing I remember saying…

CHAPTER FOUR

"Hello, friend from the Outworlds."

Those were the first words I can distinctly recall hearing after I'd awoken from my heat-induced coma. The voice was, of course, still of the young female type, as I related to you just now—well, *earlier,* at least.

At long last, my vision resumed its more-than-sharpened focus…and what a sight did *I* gaze upon as a result.

Now, before you weirdos reading this get a perverted turn of mind on this, allow me to state that this lovely young lady was indeed fully clothed. As far as I could tell, her apparel consisted of a short-sleeved floral-designed shirt, white jeans, and platform shoes of the 1970s disco variety. After all, it *is* the Time Beyond Time we're in, is it not?

Now, on to her facial and hair features: her long black hair was shoulder-length ending with those "china-doll" bangs going across her forehead. Her eyes were blackish-brown, and were ever more twinkling…which all the more matched the smile radiating from the set of perfect

teeth she was sporting at present.

I tried to stand up, and got as far as a hunched-over position when my lady rescuer-friend helped

me up to my more normal stance. Instantly a surge of relief rushed its way into my psyche, and I

felt—well, *normal*. At least, as "normal" as could be, given these really weird circumstances

that I found myself in.

"Are you all right, friend from the Outworlds?" she asked.

I was still in a weak stage, but in a quite valiant and dignified way, I tried to talk.

"Yes…I'm okay now, thank you."

My new friend smiled broadly.

"That's good. Now…" she said, "who *are* you? Not that I'm rude or crass, but--"

It took me a milli-second to reply to that, but eventually I did.

"Well, my official name is FGTR-5183, but I now call myself...*Fugitor.*"

She looked at me in quite a perplexed manner. Obviously she didn't get it at first.

"Fugitor?"

"Yes, that's right. See, I'm from another Realm of Time and Space, and well, I'm sort of like your Great Gazoo in the sense that I'm now being punished for some stupid thing or other which I'll not get into now, if that's okay with you."

"The *Great Gazoo*?!?" she said in utter confusion.

Sighing rather heavily, I looked up to the skies as if in need of a response.

"Forget it. It was a stupid reference on my part," I told her with a bit of harsh finality.

Nodding her head, she'd finally gotten the message…I hope.

"Come, my Outworld friend," she said, offering her hand to mine.

Knowing better than to offend her, I took said hand in mine, and soon set off to wherever it was that she lived. Before we got too far ahead, though, I decided to use what little bit of true logic I had left and ask her name.

"Oh, by the way, miss, I didn't quite get your name."

"It's Marlena Patricia Rodriguez. Now…what's your *real* name?"

Shrugging my shoulders, I blurted it out.

"My name, in actuality, is Tony. Just…Tony," I replied, not daring to utter my last name.

Thankfully, she didn't ask my last name.

"Hi, Tony," she said, grinning from ear to ear.

Now we can carry on, I thought to myself.

And this we thus did…

CHAPTER FIVE

We came upon a rather normal-looking town, complete with shops, restaurants, a nice play-ground (where I gazed upon a group of small children playing about on the various swing sets), and a rather out-of-place castle in the distance…with an even *more* out-of-place factory adjacent to the castle.

At that instant I knew, there and then, I was definitely *not* dreaming all this up. I mean, all the reading in the world (if you'll excuse that term) couldn't even *dare* prepare me for all of these things that I now was witnessing.

During the course of it all, Marlena turned to me, a new look of curiosity on her face.

"Now…" she asked me, "tell me where you're from."

I hesitated, not at all certain whether I should or not.

"Well?!" she hissed somewhat angrily.

Running my fingers through my greying hair, I breathed out wearily.

"Well...I'll tell you under only one condition. That you promise not to laugh. Is that understood?" I answered in a demanding manner.

"Fair enough," she said, her momentary anger dissipated.

Sighing heavily, as I'm wont to do in these circumstances, I began relating my tale.

"Well...I don't how quite to begin this, but I'll try to encapsulate this as much as humanly possible. First off, you were spot-on accurate in deducing that I'm not from this world. In fact, I'm actually from another Universe altogether...and I can assure you now that my home Universe is definitely *not* the most pleasant to live in."

Marlena opened her mouth as if to interrupt, but knew enough not to. I went on.

"Anyway, my world is ruled by the group of sentient machinery known only as the Bureaucracy. Their rather odoius task is to make damned sure that Humankind exists only to service the collective. And how is that, I can feel you ask? Well, we're assigned specific tasks in co-relation to whatever part of the Bureaucracy raised us to become. Myself, for instance, I have a rather over-inquisitive mind, so as a result, I was assigned to use my intellect to spread their smelly lies to the rest of Humankind…and I can tell you that I found this to be most distressing."

I paused, allowing Marlena to ask her question.

"But why *did* you put up with that?"

"Simply put, I literally had no choice -- well, let me re-phrase that. It was either that, or be destroyed. And I mean *that* in the literal sense. See, the Bureaucracy just doesn't tolerate dissension of any sort." I kept trying not to become angry at all this I was telling, but it was hard.

Just then, Marlena's eyes blazed in total rage.

"Then what happened?" she queried.

"Well, as Time went on, I grew to thinking about what their *real* objectives were. And thus one evening, after the work-day ended, I snuck my way into the HQ Building, downloaded the information, and received the shock of my life!!"

"And what did you discover?"

A very tense pause permeated all about us as I struggled to answer her question.

"I had found out the Bureaucracy was only a front for the vanguard of an invading group out to first subjugate and then…utterly wipe out all Humanity from the face of every Myriad World they would come into contact with. And, somewhat rashly, I told them this. In other words, I caught them with their collective pants down.

"Afterwards, they'd put me on 'trial', found me guilty, and thus sentenced me to an ageless exile roaming about the Myriad Worlds in the Universe. Then, days into my journey, well—here I am, telling you all this. Now do you believe me on all that I said?"

"Yeah, I believe you. Your story gave me the creeps, though."

"I apologize for that. But it had to be told."

Inside the recesses of my mind, a rather strange resolve wormed its way into my thinking.

Hmmm…I wonder if….

Sure!!!

CHAPTER SIX

Having just related as much as I wished to reveal to Marlena my overall sense of newness instantly began wearing itself off, and thus I found myself gradually adjusting to my new life on this hitherto unnamed planetoid. I figured by now the time had arrived to ask the name of this world.

"I say, Marlena, there's one thing I'd forgotten to ask you," I said.

"Oh? What's that?"

"Well, I'm rather grateful for your kindness and all, but I do want to know one little thing. I'm a bit curious as to the name of this planetoid we're on."

Unbelievably, she burst out in a series of small giggles.

"Oh!! I almost forgot to tell you this planet doesn't really have a name."

"What?!? Surely you jest!!"

I tried to prepare myself for her next response, as inane as it turned out.

"No, I'm dead-dog serious. And my name isn't Shirley. Sorry, but I couldn't resist," she said, laughing herself to the point of utter silliness.

Let's face it, Leslie Nielsen she definitely *wasn't.* My inner groan said as much.

"Can we just get on finding ourselves some shade and refreshments?" I wearily asked.

After her rather inane guffaw-festival subsided, we then set off.

In a few minutes we entered a nice little pub called *The Last Refuge,* sat down, requested some food and drink, and basically whittled the time away. All the while, an unusually weird tingling sensation overtook me, and I shivered as a result. It's as if…there were inside me a shrillish buzzing drone coursing its way all about my frame. I didn't know exactly *what* it was, but it really scared the hell out of me by then.

Marlena took exceptional notice of this, and grew worried.

"Tony? What's wrong?"

I didn't readily have an answer for her question, but my shaking and trembling increased, and afterwards I was about to faint when, incredibly, it ceased as suddenly as it started.

I sat back down, a cold sweat beading itself on my forehead, but otherwise I was unharmed. And, as befitting my personality, my curiosity was piqued. Such is the ways of the Universe, I suppose.

After our quick meal was finished, Marlena resumed out little tour of the area where she lived, and where I had the weird fortune of landing. Then I found my line of vision drawn to the factory in the distance. It had a sort of neo-Art Deco layout, mixed in with the look I'd seen in every science fiction story I followed.

I decided to ask Marlena outright.

"I say, Marlena, what's that factory over called?"

Without missing one single beat, she provided the answer.

"Oh, that's the famous Foxtrot Time Works. It keeps everything here in what we call the Temporal Balance."

Aha!! Now I understood.

"And, uh, who actually *runs* the factory?" I queried.

"Well, as far as I know, it's supervised by a Mr. Steve Hackett."

My jaw dropped down to the ground in utter disbelief!!!

"Did you just actually say -- *Steve Hackett?!?*"

Marlena gazed at me in peculiar manner.

"Why, yeah, I did. Why do you ask?"

I hesitated in responding, again as I'm wont to do at times such as this.

"Oh…no reason at all. No reason."

CHAPTER SEVEN

Day after day, my stay here grew increasingly boring, drab, and tedious and for the first time ever in my life, I was actually *craving* for a bit of adventurous excitement…if only to just break the monotony of it all, I suppose.

With Marlena at my side, however, that little thought had to be put on the proverbial back-burner for the nonce. I just couldn't risk her safety. Yet somehow, I got that same sense of adventurous rebellion in *her*.

Risking all manners of decency, I turned to her.

"I say, Marlena, may I ask of you a rather…*personal* question?"

"Sure," she replied.

I breathed heavily trying my damnedest best to weigh my words carefully.

"Do you -- oh, how am I to say this? -- *enjoy* your life here?"

Without a moment's hesitation, she made her answer be known.

"No, not really. I mean, it's so *dull* here overall."

I couldn't help but smile at that one.

"*Really?!!*" I shouted out.

She looked at me in her trademark wary manner.

"Just what do you have in *mind?!*"

I humorously wiggled my greying eyebrows, my smile ever present by this time.

"Oh…nothing *too* dangerous, I should think."

Marlena's wariness slowly melted like snow in Phoenix, Arizona.

"And, uh, how are we *going* to have this little sojourn you're planning?!"

She made the most valid point imaginable. I hadn't thought of that.

"Well?!" she asked persistently.

"Oh, I bloody well don't know," I uttered out in frustration. And with that said, a fly commenced buzzing about my head, driving me batty. As I swiped at the filthy little degenerate, a weird stream of light swept its way into our collective vision. I gingerly repeated the motion, and the light-stream magnified in its dimensions…and also allowed us a minute glimpse into another place, totally unlike our present location.

Our jaws dropped in utter shock!!

We turned to each other, reading one another's minds in regards to the visions.

"Shall we?" I asked in a bold if somewhat slightly crass manner.

"Let's do it."

And thus we two, Marlena and I, set off into the Unknown…

CHAPTER EIGHT

Times beyond times, worlds upon worlds, Realms and other Realms greeted us upon our rapid

departure from Marlena's home in the now-drab Time Beyond Time. Somehow or other, I

sensed that Marlena was welcoming this as much as I.

A new surge of omnipotence surged its way all about my being as my confidence in my just-

discovered power increased exponentially. In fact, I began formulating a rather ominous plan in

the deepest recesses of my mind…but, for the sake of decency and good manners, I dared not

utter them out loud lest I risk frightening Marlena out of her senses. Then again, maybe it was

for the best that she learn about this sooner or later, I suppose.

Anyway, we grew quite fascinated by the various galaxy clusters that met our eyes. Star-system

after star-system sped by, and we witnessed more and more of the Myriad Worlds, some of which

were in the process of chaotic formation, and some of which, unfortunately, were on a rather sad

decline till their time of demise. In a sense, it was as if we were touring the very Essence of Life

itself.

Oh…I'll bet you're wondering how we managed to stay alive and breathing throughout endless,

airless Space, aren't you? Well, it's relatively simple enough. See, when we departed the Realm of the Time Beyond Time, I had the good fortune of using my power (which, I'm glad to say, was in limitless supply) to create a force-field barrier about our forms. *And*...we also purchased some food and drink to sustain ourselves. (I have to apologize to you for neglecting to tell you much sooner.)

Just then, Marlena unexpectedly turned 'round to me.

"Tony!! Look down there!" she yelled, pointing downward.

I followed her direction, and there below us I gazed upon one of the most weirdest sights I'd ever encountered in all my years of living. Below our vantage point was a majestic, gigantic city-ship—well, *fortress-ship,* actually. Quite massive, and armed to the nines with humongous lasers, photon cannons, defense screen-shields, shock-wave deflectors, and sundry other machines of power!! What its *purpose* was, well, I couldn't dare try to even make a half-baked guess. I'd more than likely be wrong, anyway.

A look of fear crossed Marlena's lovely young face.

"What if whoever's in there sees us?"

In reply, I thrust my right arm out forward, and willed our speed to increase itself to eight times the speed of light (which, in case you were unaware, is exactly 186,525 miles per second). Our bodies felt just the *Millenium Falcon*, going at that rate of velocity. It did nothing for our eyesight, though, seeing those stars just whiz by in the manner that they did.

A sense of relief, not unlike the feeling one gets upon drinking Alka-Seltzer for upset stomach, washed over us, and thus I reduced our speed, allowing us to resume our rather semi-leisurely tour of the Myriad Worlds, hopeful that we wouldn't encounter any further sudden dangers.

At least, that was our plan, anyway…

CHAPTER NINE

For monemt after moment, our journey through the Myriad Worlds carried on, with nary a surprise or shock from the outside forces of Utter Chaos. All in all, it was enjoyable if somewhat a little on the dull, routine side of it all.

In fact, it grew a tad bit on the boring side of it all. Marlena made *that* point known.

"How much longer is this going to last?" she moaned.

For once, I didn't have a ready-made answer. I knew as much as she did by this stage, which is to say not very much. And let me be the first to say that it began to worry the hell out of us by this stage, so as a result, I didn't dare bring the subject up any further…at least, until we know more, at any rate.

Soon afterwards, her boredom was replaced by a new surge of delighted curiosity.

"Tony, look over there!!" she said loudly.

"Where?" I asked, looking about.

In a rather forceful manner, Marlena grabbed my head, and swiveled it to an even stranger sight than the gigantic fortress-ship we'd avoided (barely). For just to our right, we caught a glimpse of a monolithic planet, eight times the size of Jupiter in our own mundane Solar System…and it was *dividing itself!!!* It's as if the planet was a giant amoeba…and, more to the point, it looked *hungry,* though we really couldn't confirm that for certain.

We turned to one another, our jaws dropping!!

"What do we do now?" asked Marlena.

I shook my head, once more not having a ready-made reply to her question.

Then, inexplicably, Marlena's face brightened, her eyes popping in delight.

"I've got it!! Tony, can you try to do one those 'mind-melds'?"

A look of bafflement crossed my slightly-aged face.

"A mind-meld?! Who do I look like, *Leonard Nimoy*?!??!"

"Well, it wouldn't hurt now, would it?" she asked unperturbedly.

Not wanting to hurt her feelings, and like an idiot, I stretched out my arms in the direction of the "creature"…where, frighteningly enough, I got an actual response!! And *what* a response did I get!!

"*Well, hello there*," it "said" in a voice not unlike Leslie Nielsen.

"Hello there, yourself," I responded back, trying to remain somwhat civil in spite of my own in-credulous reaction to these weird events.

Marlena just couldn't what she was now witnessing.

"I don't believe it!! It really *worked!!*" she gasped.

Not heeding her any mind, I did my best to resume my conversation with our contact.

"What are you called?" I asked the "creature".

"Well…I'm not really sure about my name. See, uh, I don't get around very much. In fact, you're the very first -- what are you called? -- humans I've met."

"Well, for the sake of good manners, allow me to introduce myself. I am called Fugitor, though my actual name is Tony. And this," I said, now turning to my traveling companion, "is my friend Marlena."

The "creature" throbbed about, as though it was excited to see a female human…in fact, *any* human, as it—oh, let's call it "he" from here-in-on—just said scant moments ago.

"Hi, there. Say, is there a reason why you sound like the actor Leslie Nielsen?" uttered Marlena.

My eyeballs rolled up in disgust at *that* one, believe me. Then, incredibly enough, the "creature" actually *laughed* uproariously in delighted joy.

"Leslie Nielsen!! Oh, that's a good *one, miss!"* he said as he continued giggling. *"Well, miss, you just gave me my new name. Leslie it is. Thanks, uh, Marlena, was it?"*

"Yeah, that's right," said Marlena, in smug satisfaction.

I didn't quite believe what I actually saw occur. I mean, how often do you encounter a gigantic amoebic creature, discover that his voice resembles a comedic actor, and get thanked for giving such a creature the name of said comedic actor?? The answer: rarely to never. At least not in the usual circumstances, anyway.

But…in a very strange manner, I had to hand it to Marlena. She knew how to make friends rather easily if somewhat illogically.

Not that I'm complaining, mind…

CHAPTER TEN

After a few days -- well, at least, what *passed* for days in this otherwise timeless Realm, we had decided to take our leave. The only problem: what to do with Leslie, the giant amoeboid to whom we'd grown somewhat attached. We couldn't just abandon him to a unending exile with no outside contact what-so-ever.

For a few -- actually, *several* minutes, we mulled the idea over and over in our minds. Then, not to my unfortunate surprise, Marlena made up our minds for us.

"Hey, Tony, let's take Leslie *with* us!"

I turned 'round to her, in utter anger.

"Have you gone daft, girl?!! How can we take along a giant amoeba?!! My power isn't *that* limitless, I hope you know!!"

Somehow or other, Leslie managed to sense this.

"Well, I think *I may have a plan. Here goes...*EYAAAAHHH!!!" With that, Leslie had, weirdly

enough, actually *reduced* his size down to that of a balloon.

Now our conumdrum was solved.

"Shall we all go?" he asked.

In the recesses of my mind, I was still in a state of uninhibited shock and awe!

"Surely you just did the impossible?!"

"Yeah, that's right. And don't call me Shirley."

Not wanting to fall victim to any more of these rather outmoded and outdated puns, I putforth

my will-power and thus set off; imagine this rather madcap trio of myself, Marlena, and Leslie

the Amoeboid Comic. Oh well. No one said that friendship had to be logical, right?

In an instant, the stars resumed their swiftness as our velocity once more increased to now more than twelve times the speed of light. Worlds beyond worlds opened up, and times beyond times came and went like a summer breeze. In our little force-field screen-sphere, we three carried on a mundane and happy conversation.

Naturally, Marlena asked another of her rather inane questions.

"What did you do for entertainment?"

Leslie mulled about this for only a milli-second.

"Well…I sub-divide myself on occasion, and then I re-form back to one form just to break up the monotony of the whole damn thing. Believe me, it's no picnic. Oh, speaking of which, got a box of grub handy? I'm starved."

I creased my forehead, trying to come up with a somewhat viable solution to that.

Then…of course. It hit me a bit on the sudden side of it all.

"Why don't we head back to *The Last Refuge* and get some nourishment to go? I'm sure we can all agree to that, surely."

"*Sounds good. And stop calling us Shirley,*" replied Leslie. I fell for it once more, much to my immediate chagrin if not anger.

And so, again, I put forth my will-power and set our course back to the Realm of the Time Beyond Time, that rather drab existance we'd left long times gone. But then again, that's the beauty of time-space travel, I suppose.

Only we emphatically *didn't* know what was lying in wait for us...

CHAPTER ELEVEN

Once more, worlds upon worlds, times and more times, and one Realm after another raced by at a constant rate of velocity, and we three grew ever so fascinated by the sheer amazed wonder of the Mysteries of the Universe, leaving us totally speechless as a result. In Marlena's case, that was a good thing, as I could no longer tolerate any more of her idiotic questions and crass remarks.

I mean, I don't wish to sound ungrateful to her, and I certainly would like for our friendship to endure, but, well, to be honest, unlike my powers, my patience had rapidly reached its limits to the Nth degree. But again, either out of good manners or out of sheer if slight cowardice on my part, I dared not utter those thoughts out loud lest I risk losing that friendship.

Then, oddly, she turned 'round to me, her eyes watering slightly. I, of course, didn't like that one iota, and it became worrying to see this…especially with Leslie tagging about.

"I say, Marlena, are you all right?" I asked.

She didn't readily reply at first. *Now* I grew even more concerned.

"Yeah…I'm okay, Tony," she meekly answered.

I pressed the issue a tad further.

"Are you really?"

Then it came out. The truthful answer, that is.

"No, I'm not all right!! In fact, I'm never going to *be* all right!!"

"Oh? And why's that, I ask?"

A tense pause permeated all about us as she tried to carefully respond.

"It's *you!!* All right?! It's you!! You don't really *like* me, do you?!"

That little revelation quite stunned me, to say the least of it all.

"Of course I like you. I mean, you literally saved my life when I landed on your world. It's just that, well—oh, God, how am I to say this?—you *do* tend to ask questions that are a smidgeon on the silly side. But that's part of your charm, I suppose." Now I had done it!!

"No, Tony, that's not what's bothering me. I know I say wacky things, but as you said, that *is* part of my charm. I meant you don't...well, to be frank, you don't *love* me, do you?"

Now *that* shocked me almost to no end. But she did have a valid point. It's just that I didn't escape an Eternal Exile only to find romance with a young and, admittedly, attractive woman I'd just only met moments upon arrival.

At that precise state, Leslie finally said a few words.

"Uhh...aren't we getting our food?" he asked nonchalantly.

Turning my gaze about, I looked at him, my expression on the somber side.

"Yes…we'll get some food."

I said little to nothing afterwards.

CHAPTER TWELVE

An uneasy silence cascaded about us as the journey back to the Time Beyond Time neared its

conclusion. Not one of us, I need remind you, said a single word and it worried all of us, believe

me on that, my friends. If there's one thing I despise (besides my former masters-turned-

archenemies), it's good friendships turning sour.

Upon landing on the spot near the pub, the three of us exited the force-field screen now dissolved

from all about us. The silence grew even more deafening, if that's at all possible.

Just before entering the pub, Marlena unexpectedly walked up to me, a look of apologetic guilt

marking her attractive features.

"Tony...I want you to know that what I said to you, I didn't really mean it. For that, I'm deeply

sorry," she told me, as though trying to lift a burden off her shoulders.

I didn't know what, or indeed, *how* to respond. Romantic feelings, like true logic, was not one

on my strongest suits in this card game called Life, insofar as I know.

"Well . . . " I began stating, somewhat hesitantly, "let's just let it drift away, at least for the nonce anyway." And with that said, all seemed forgiven -- I hope.

After quickly entering the pub, purchasing our nourishment, and then exiting, we wordlessly resumed our journey—well, not straight away. And why's that, you ask me? Well, rather from out of the blue, Leslie(whom I'd momentarily forgotten about) floated about to my face. I didn't know this (what with him being an amoeboid and all), but it grew apparent that he was cross (that's angry, in another word) with my handling of the situation between Marlena and myself.

*"Say, Tony, I noticed that you kind of gave your girl the...*brush-off, *is it?"* he said.

I whirled 'round, trying a little too hard to remain calm about this.

"Look, Leslie, it isn't that I don't like Marlena. In fact, I like her almost to the point that I'm starting to -- " I began, then stopped myself.

"Aha!! I think, Tony, you're starting to fall in love her. Isn't that right, Mr. Wishy-Willy? Well?"

Having uttered that to my face, he throbbed about in what was, to me, a case of the most smug-gest satisfaction imaginable.

I was more than prepared to make a rebuttal when the words sunk in.

After a brief pause, I realized, to my dismay, that Leslie was spot-on accurate. I *was* falling for her, but I didn't wish to admit that. Not even to myself.

But I had to tell her my truest feelings lest I further risk alienating her from me. And *that*, my friends, is another thing about Life that I'll not tolerate, thank you so very much.

And thus, drawing a heavy breath, I made my move…

CHAPTER THIRTEEN

"Marlena!!!" I called out loudly.

Not surprisingly, she turned her way 'round to me. She wasn't angry, but her demeanor definitely didn't show any sign of warm, fuzzy friendliness what-so-ever.

"What do you want now, Tony?"

I remained on the calm side of the issue, but I had to move forth with my resolve.

"We need to have a chat. Now," I firmly said.

Shrugging her shoulders in weary resignation, she eyed my English features intently.

"Okay, Tony, let's chat." Her tone of voice was quite cold, to say the least. To say the most, it was quite harsh, albeit somewhat incongruous coming from such a lovely young woman.

Swiftly, though not in my usual manner, oddly, I got straight on to the point.

"I know what's been depressing you, and I wish for you to know that, well -- oh, God, how am I to tell you this? -- I really *am* beginning to like you immensely. In fact -- oh, here it comes -- I'm actually becoming rather attracted to you. I just didn't want to admit that, because of my outer demeanor, and the type of personality I am. I do hope you can understand all this."

I didn't readily notice this at first, but her old happy-go-lucky demeanor had rapidly coursed her way throughout her features. Then...she sped up to me, and with a cry of joyous relief, commenced to embrace the living stuffings out of me, and then planted a rather passionate kiss on my mouth. What's even more strange is that, well—I actually *welcomed* it!

After a few minutes of this unexpected love story, Leslie floated his way 'round to us.

"Ahem. Sorry to interrupt your little Erich Segal moment, but...shouldn't we got going before too long? Oh, by the way thanks for taking my advice, Tony."

Marlena looked at me perplexedly.

"Who's Erich Segal?" she asked

"It's a long story -- oh, damn. Look, Leslie's right. We should go."

And so, having gotten as prepared as much as humanly possible, we then set off on the next, and hopefully drab, part of our sojourn. Once more, I re-formed the force-field screen about ourselves, and in a zip of time we found ourselves airborne, then…*space*-borne!

As I stated scant moments ago, I hoped the next part was routine.

Of course, as these things usually go, *that* little wish would definitely *not* come to be…

CHAPTER FOURTEEN

Well into the new journey, we once more saw stars whiz by at the usual rate of hyper-velocity, and only did a new and even weirder sight than Leslie coming to our view did we slow down and ultimately cease speed altogether.

And just what *was* that unusual phemonenon, you ask?

Well, it seems that we stumbled upon what appeared to be a…gaseous *bubble* of some sort. In a rather silly manner, it reminded me of something I'd seen on the old *Space: 1999* vid-prog back on my home-world, in my tiny apartment.

We were all aghast with utter amazement.

"Tony…it's so *beautiful!*" gasped Marlena.

Next it was Leslie's turn to respond. Only *his* response was a tad—well, see for yourself.

"Hey, cousin Ted!! Still off your diet, huh? Well, that's life," he said.

I couldn't help smile at that one, though I knew that it was only a gas sphere. It just sat there, not moving, only reflecting the lights from the countless stars gathered all about it. That reflected light made its way into our force-field screen, making it seem like one of those disco nightclubs that were so prevalent on Old Earth, way back in the Ancient Times called the 1970s. And no, it did most emphatically *not* make us feel like dancing, thank you so very much.

Much to our surprise, that disco-feeling would be rather a bit on the moot side. For just then, the gaseous sphere we were so drawn to had somehow contracted itself, and then…actually grew to a gigantic size; in fact, it was expanding itself to a size that was, I'd say, at least *twelve times* greater than that of the Sun in your Solar System. Only it didn't stop there!! That initial size increased exponentially, almost to the breaking strain!

Inside our force-field screen, a wave of fear permeated its way all around us!

"Tony, what's *happenning?!?!*" screeched out Marlena.

"Uh, Tony, don't you think we should, you know, leave right now?" asked Leslie.

Before I could make my move, the gas sphere had finally reached its total breaking point!

Then…*utter Cataclysm!!*

To our surprise and shock, the damned sphere utterly ruptured, sending out a powerful force of energy headed straight in our direction…and there was little to be done about it!

Now that wave of gave way to total panic if not all-out terror!!

"Tony, *do* something!! ANYTHING!!" yelled out Marlena.

Like an idiot, I put forth all the will-power I was able to muster, but as I had realized moments ago, I could do very little to stop this! There was no way, however, that I would ever dare think to disappoint Leslie or especially Marlena.

For agonizing moment after agonizing moment, I struggled to keep ourselves alive if not fully safe and sound. I mean, this isn't *quite* what I was cut out for in life, was it? I realized then that the more I fought, the more greater the danger grew.

Onwards and onwards we traversed, into times beyond times beyond times, and by the endless Myriad Worlds, just straight on; one after the other, some in birth and some in total demise. And some worlds we saw -- well, those I can leave up to all our collective imaginations and not even dare try to logically describe.

Basically, though, the most easiest way to put it: Douglas Trumbull, eat your heart out!

Slowly, our fear, panic, and terror melted away as they were replaced by a growing sense of total awe and utter if not strange delight. And these new and diverse variations of the Myriad Worlds were ours for the taking...not that we're power-hungry, you understand.

Finally, our increased velocity actually reduced itself, and we found ourselves cruising about at a much more leisurely pace, to our combined relief.

We commenced looking about at the new sights that greeted our eyes. For once, even Leslie (whom I had always a tendency to inadvertantly neglect at times) was rendered speechless by the wonders that befell us.

After that, it all settled back down into a nice if somewhat abbreviatedly casual road trip into the vast reaches of the Universe. Then to Marlena's astonishment, she saw a star-system that she'd never encounterd before, pointing to a blue-green planetoid in the third orbit about the center Sun.

"Hey, Tony, what planet is *that,* I wonder?"

I looked downward, and much to my overt chagrin and anger combined, I realized that we'd found ourselves in my home star-system!! Seeing this really set my teeth on edge!!

Leslie floated his way to me, then backed off. I think somehow or other, he knew.

My plan for Justice was still very much in the recesses of my mind, yet I felt unready to execute it as such. Especially not with my two comrades in tow. I'd no intention of placing their lives in utter Danger just so I could gain a little vengeance for myself. If I did, I'd never live with my-self, I thought.

With their welfare at the forefront of my mind, I turned 'round to them.

"What say we leave here?" I asked.

Not surprisingly, they agreed . . . for the nonce, anyway.

CHAPTER FIFTEEN

A growing surge of curiosity made its way into both Marlena's and Leslie's collective psyches, even though they were, as I stated before, agreeable about leaving my home star-system for the moment. But out of good manners on their part, they didn't utter those thoughts out loud at first.

Within a few minutes -- well, as I keep mentioning, what passed for minutes out here in Timeless Space, Marlena finally made her mind be known.

"Hey, Tony, why did you want to leave this star-system in such a hurry?"

I didn't answer at first, again out of either manners or cowardice on my part. Drawing a heavy breath, I carefully measured my words as I made my move.

"Marlena…the *real* reason we left in a dash like that is because you just caught a glance at my home world, which, I'm sure I told you before, is ruled by the Bureaucracy. And…well, I didn't wish to reveal this to you, but I'm already formulating a plot to wipe out the Bureaucracy, totally, swiftly, and I dare say, *violently!!* I only kept that part from you out of worry for your safety—well, yours and Leslie's. I do hope you're in a forgiving way upon knowing this."

She said not one word, as if she had to gauge her own reaction to this news.

Then, to my relieved delight, she once more embraced the stuffings out of my frame.

And of course, as usual Leslie interrupted us.

"Uh, say, uh, Tony, don't look now, but -- " he said.

The three of us whirled about, and got a rather sudden jolt of a surprise. There, within our vantage point, was the very same gigantic fortress-ship we'd encountered much, much earlier in our voyages. Incredibly, it had somehow or other spotted us, and was even now racing its way in order to capture us!!

"Hang on, all!! It's going to get a tad bit BUMPY!!!"

In a quick instant, I drew all the will-power I was able to muster, and tried desperately to increase our velocity to almost *twenty times* the speed of light. To my dismay, the fortress-ship activated what I deduced to be one of those "tractor-beams" that one oft-times associates with science fiction films. But, I can attest to you know that *this* wasn't science fiction!!

This was real, and this was getting *deadly!!*

Panic permeated all about us!

"Tony!! Do something!!!" yelled out Marlena.

Again like an idiot, I did as she requested, but the damned tractor-beam was too powerful and it was all I could do to remain conscious in the midst of my struggle!

"Marlena…I can't go on like this. Too…strong," I gasped out in agony.

She nodded, and thus the three of us soon found ourselves drawn right to the heart, or brain, if you will, of the fortress-ship. My agony was replaced by a growing fascination with the ship, as a flood of questions entered my mind…for which we would get answers in a weird way.

CHAPTER SIXTEEN

Upon entering the fortress-ship, we disembarked out of the force-field screen, and commenced exploring about the more immediate area. All around we gazed at all sorts of highly advanced technological wonderment. Whoever built this, I mused to myself, must have been a genius, to say the least.

We were about to enter a doorway in our path, just a tad to our left, when a loud, somewhat authoritative voice put a halt...and that very said voice was like that of Jack Webb himself!

"All right, son, that's far enough. You can't go any further."

"Who are you?" I asked rather harshly.

"Well, son, that's a long story, but I can't take the time to go into just yet. First things first. Now...how did you get in here?"

I was a bit reluctant to answer, but with Marlena and Leslie with me, it was for the best that I do so.

"Well, you see, we were caught in your tractor-beam, and that's how we entered your ship." I felt confident the reply would satisfy the "man" in charge. Not to my surprise, it obviously didn't do the job.

"Oh, really? Well, let me ask you this, son. Where's your ship at? We didn't detect any vessel that had you in it."

"Oh, that. Well, it *is* a rather long tale, but suffice it to say to you that -- well, we don't have one. Rather strange, don't you agree?"

The guard-machine paused in its casualistic interrogation.

"How do you mean, 'strange'?"

I smiled slightly as I prepared my next answer.

"Well, see, I created a force-field screen 'round my companions and I, by total mind-power alone. No machinery needed, if that can be believed."

The "voice" paused once more, as though rendering a verdict of some sort.

"Well, son, in this day and age, with all the things we've seen and heard, I'd be willing to believe just about anything at this rate. Okay, you didn't come here to attack us. You're welcome to stay if you wish."

"Thank you so very kindly. We might just do that. Oh, by the way, before I forget my manners, allow me to introduce ourselves. My name's Tony, alias Fugitor, and these are my friends Leslie the Amoeboid, and Marlena Patricia Rodriguez."

"Glad to meet you all. I'm Friday, as I gather you know from the sound of my voice."

We all had a smile at that.

"We're glad to meet you, Friday," said Marlena.

"Say, uh, Friday, how did you *get here?"* inquired Leslie.

Friday acted as though he was afraid to respond…or at least, unwilling to do so.

"Well…as much as I can tell, I was built here by the Star-Guild. It's a group of worlds not unlike a police force. Their job is to make sure that all of the Myriad Worlds are protected and kept from Chaos, Anarchy, Warfare, and Destruction. To that end, they constructed a fleet of fortress-ships, myself included."

"And where is the Star-Guild now?" I asked.

"Yeah, where?" interjected Marlena, her fascination for Friday's tale growing.

Friday sighed sadly, if that's at all possible for a sentient fortress-ship.

"Well, you see, an armada from the Nether Regions called the Hyradians tried to, and succeeded in, invading the galaxy where the Myriad Worlds were. All fortress-ships were called in to defend our galaxy, and soon a terrible war ensued. Tragically, some of the Myriad Worlds met a very horrific end, while the rest valiantly struggled to ward off the Hyradians.

"Victory was, of course, achieved, but the price was all too high. The Star-Guild was no longer willing to allow their ships to be used, much less summoned, for such grim purposes again. As a result, all the sentient fortress-ships were decomissioned, and made to orbit at various points throughout the Galaxies of the Universe. You're talking to the only one left still running at full maximum function. A sad tale, isn't it?"

It was indeed a sad tale, if ever I've heard one.

CHAPTER SEVENTEEN

A thought entered Marlena's mind as Friday finished relating his lonely story.

"Hey, Tony, I've got an idea," she said, turning 'round to me. "Let's take Friday with us. He'd be a good bodyguard, and plus it'll be good for Leslie as well."

This time I felt she'd totally lost her mind. As I'm sure I told her, and you, before, my power *was* limitless…but even limitlessness, I dare say, has its, well, limits.

"Say, that's not a bad idea. What do you think, Tony?"

Again, that sense of reluctance gnawed its way into my brain.

"Well…I don't know. It'd be awfully difficult, lugging Friday's massive frame about throughout Limitless Space and Time."

For a short spell, no one uttered a single word. Then, weirdly enough, Friday had a bright notion.

"You know what? I can help. See, I didn't tell you this out of my own carelessness, but I can use the hydra-thrusters on the aft side of my structure. Its power supply is more limitless than even your own powers. That way, you can save your energy for whatever it is you have to do. And...I don't have to worry about food or drink or anything like that. Besides that, I'm not really doing much of anything else anyway. So what do you say, friend? Is it a go?"

I didn't need to take a long moment to answer.

"Okay, sure. Why not?"

And we all cheered like we'd never, ever cheered before.

Soon after that, however, that same old problem arose in my psyche.

"I say, Friday, I'm all for the plan and all, but I don't know if you're aware of this fact or not, but I can travel not only in Space but in Time as well. And, well—I'm not at all certain if you're up to the many sojourns through Time. Plus, it'd be a massive drain on my powers. That's the one -- well, the *chief* problem."

Friday mulled over this dilemma for only a fraction of a milli-second.

"Say, that's not a problem. I've already thought of that. I can harness a smidgeon of your power; thus, I can duplicate it. Let me have your hand." And with that having been said, Friday opened a small compartment on his control-console panel. I put my hand on the sensor for only a few seconds.

When those few seconds elapsed, I released my hand from the energy sensor, not feeling drained in the slightest bit at all. In fact, if not anything I felt my powers actually *increase* to even more loftier levels, if that's at all possible.

"Okay, I've done analysis, and the harnessing process is already in motion. I should have the power in my system shortly."

Within a short pause, Friday's processing was completed. I have to say to you that I was rather impressed, to say the least. To say the most, I was almost frightened!

Then, finally, we prepared to set off…but not before Leslie made one of his rather illogically crass puns be heard.

"Say, if you're Friday, what happened to all the other days of the week?"

It was indeed fortunate that Friday had the sense not to respond…but I couldn't say the same for Marlena or myself, as my inner groan declared.

"Look, can we get on? I don't wish to stay a bit longer, if that can be helped."

All agreed, and finally -- *finally!* -- we set off, with Friday about to take the grandest journey of his entire life-time…

CHAPTER EIGHTEEN

Once more, worlds and worlds, times beyond times, and star-system after star-system raced by at the usual velocity beyond the speed of light. Much to my surprise, Friday kept up with us with no trouble what-so-ever. I had to hand it to him: he showed absolutely no sign of trepidation or fear. But of course, he's just a machine…at least, that's what I *believed* at the time, anyway.

I knew that it'd be somewhat on the silly side of it all, but I decided to ask Friday a rather mundane question, much to my companions' bemusement if not utter confusion.

"I say, Friday, how do like your first sojourn through the Myriad Worlds?"

"Oh, it's great, son. Wouldn't miss this for anything," he replied, not missing a beat.

"Yes, I know what you mean by that."

Then Marlena turned her lovely gaze 'round to me.

"I don't know about you, but I'm *starved!* Can we stop and eat for a little bit?"

Unexpectedly a rather malodorous stench greeted our noses. It emanated from our resident cheap punster-amoeboid.

"Uh, sorry about that, but I forgot to tell you that when I don't consume food—well, you can smell for yourself. I do hope you understand, don't you?"

Unfortunately for myself…I did, and so we found a small planetoid, roughly the size and area of Jellystone Park. In a few moments we made contact, with us three flesh-and-blood units landing on the surface, and Friday orbiting about the planet's outer rim in stationary position. A twinge of guilt froze us momentarily as we left Friday's point. But if he felt a sense of abandonment, he didn't show it in the slightest bit.

Our meal thus ended, we four resumed our sojourn, which by then had, for the first time ever, fallen into a welcome if mundane trip. I suppose that it was a bit like Life itself.

But…I should have known that like everything else I'd seen up to this point, that mudane feeling wouldn't last all that much longer. For you see, the moment we left the galactic answer to Jellystone behind, our eyes were met by a rather hideous (in the moral sense) sight. It came in the form of a gigantic airship, armed with lasers and defense-screens all about. Two high-grade engine-nacelles, sleek and aerodynamic, were positioned on either side of the ship's aft side.

"What do you suppose that type of airship is, Friday?" I asked.

Friday didn't readily respond. When he did, however, the reply wasn't pleasant!

"That, I'm sorry to say, is a Hyradian airship. I fought one like this before, and I have no wish to engage in a battle, especially now with your lives in my care." His devotion to our welfare was greatly welcomed, but we knew it'd be a moot point if we didn't do something to escape the Hyradian airship's path!!

Marlena was hit by an idea!

"Hey, Friday, why don't you send out one of those warning salvos? That way, no one gets hurt in any way."

"That's a great idea, Marlena, but there's only one major problem with that."

"Oh? What's that?" she asked.

"The Hyradians are perhaps the most merciless *race of humans I had ever encountered. They don't care about anything or anyone but their own goals in life."*

"So. It's either the tiger or the tiger," I said.

"Looks that way, doesn't it?"

A tense pause permeated once more about us as Friday contemplated a course of action.

Reluctantly Friday made his decision.

"Okay, I guess I don't have any more choice, do I?"

With that now said, Friday executed his plan. Having ordered us into his massive infra-structure(which was, fortunately for us, rigged with an autonomously-programmed force-field), he let loose with a barrage of photon torpedoes, laser-blasts, and shock-wave thrusts…all the while making every effort to detect any signs of Life. Again, his concern for life was admirable, yet, in this case, somewhat irrelevant.

And, you ask, why is that irrelevant?

Well, much to his surprise, the detectors found out that the Hyradian airship was totally devoid of everything biological. In other words, there was no one in it!!

We couldn't believe it, much less understand it all!!

After the battle ceased, Friday scanned inside the infra-structure to check for damage.

"Is everyone all right in there?" he asked worriedly.

"Yeah, we're good, Friday. How are you?" responded Marlena.

"Oh, I'm okay. A little shaken up, that's all. And even relieved now that my short fight's over."

He *sounded* relieved, at that.

"Wow. Talk about a rockin' Friday, huh?" quipped Leslie. We all chuckled heartily.

Now we can get on, I summarized in my mind…

CHAPTER NINETEEN

Feeling none the worse for wear after that slight, if intense, battle(which, in fact, was more *fasci-nating* rather than terrifying, I must say), we found ourselves thrusting into a Realm of the Universe that we'd never encountered before. The shapes of this realm's planets were a tad *unusual,* to say the least. To say the most, it was mind-blowing!!

And why do I say that, you're wondering?

Well…for starters, some of those planets had a distinctly cuboid-shape, like seeing square boxes floating about aimlessly. Others resembled the Great Pyramids of Ancient Egypt on Old Earth, and the rest were just too amazing for me to try to describe here for your benefit, so as a result, I'll leave off trying, thank you so very much.

Out of sheer habit, Friday made a cursory scan-check for any signs of Life. None was found, due to the fact that he reported the planets' total composition to be -- hold onto your chairs, my friends -- *metallically structured!!*

The three of us, namely myself, Leslie, and Marlena gaped in utter shock!!

"How did they *get* here, if there's no life in this Realm?" asked Marlena.

"*Say, that's right, huh?*" echoed Leslie.

This was a valid point, so I mulled over this for a spot of time. Unfortunately, no answer came racing into my mind. Needless to say, I was totally baffled by this!

Not one sound from us emanated all about as this thought doggedly spun its way 'round and 'round the recesses of our minds. The silence grew almost literally deafening, threatening our very collective sanity.

Then...we heard it!!

The most unusual sound ever uttered!!

"What's that I'm hearing?" asked Marlena.

In reply, I turned 'round to Friday.

"Can you identify that sound for us?" I requested.

"Already on it."

A tense pause, possibly the most tense ever felt, chilled our spines even as Friday scanned about

the immediate perimeter, searching for the origin point of the odd sound.

Suddenly the answer came to me, like the lightning bolt of Shazam!

"Unless I'm sorely mistaken, that sounds like -- a *child's laugh!!*" I declared firmly.

Marlena's jaw dropped as though it weighed a thousand tons!

Friday's scan confirmed this notion!

"Yep, you're right, Tony. That is indeed a child's laugh. Sounds like a two-year-old girl, unless I miss my guess."

Leslie had been rendered utterly speechless during the course of this discovery. If ever we needed his wit, it was now!

But...much to disappointment, it wouldn't be forthcoming. Everything grew too overwhelming by this state, I must tell you.

For moment after moment we looked around, checking for whatever else was inevitably to come next...and sure enough, it did!!

"Tony!! Look!!!" screeched Marlena, her face wide-eyed in terror.

Presently I whirled 'round, and there, before my very eyes, was a little girl...albeit approxmately twelve stories high, with hands as gigantic as a tractor-trailer! In spite of her massive size, I must say she was rather cute.

We surmised that she was at least two years old, by human standards. (Note that I said "human standards.") Her huge eyes were brown and sparkling, her hair was black and close-cropped to her shoulders, and her garb consisted of a red dress with white collar, white pull-up tights, and black dress shoes.

As I just said earlier, she was cute, almost bubbly. She smiled constantly, having just found herself a new toy or two, maybe three…namely us!

At that moment, that familiar malodorous stench from Leslie floated its way to our noses.

"Don't tell me you're hungry again, Leslie," I said, distractedly.

His coloring was a bit on the red side.

"Well…there's at least one more thing I neglected to say."

"Oh? What's that?" I asked.

He paused in a state of embarassment.

"Well...see, I also let off a smell when I'm scared or nervous from anything new or weird, as I'm sure you just noticed."

Now he tells us, I thought in seething anger. But I couldn't do much about that now.

For you see, our troubles suddenly magnificd...and I do mean *magnified!!!*

CHAPTER TWENTY

A new and more stranger sight now met our gazes. Right behind the gigantic two-year-old baby stepped another gigantic female, this one at ten times the height of the baby. I didn't wish to say it like this, but in a way it reminded me of the very ancient vid-prog called *Land of the Giants,* which, I'm sure, most if not all of you readers are familiar with.

The baby turned 'round, her smile still on her face.

This even larger giant picked up the baby, and held her lovingly.

We flew our way to a position to see the giant woman much more accurately. She was a young red-haired woman, evidently in her late teens to early-twenties, if that's feasible. She was wearing a paisley-striped sweater with button-down shirt underneath, a long skirt, and brown zip-up platform boots. Her eyes were blue, and her smile perky and bright, not unlike the baby she now held.

What we heard and saw next -- well, see for yourself:

"Well, little lady, there you are. Time for your nap-nap," said the young "woman."

Instantly the baby turned, and tried to grab Friday from his position, but the "woman," no doubt her mother, calmly carried the baby away.

After a short spell of time, the young woman made her way back to us.

"I'm so sorry for my daughter. She's harmless," she said, looking down at us.

"Oh, it's nothing, really. By the way, your little girl's cute. What's her name?" I asked.

"Sarah. Her name's Sarah," said the young mother, smiling.

"Oh, before I forget my own manners, allow me to introduce my friends. This is Marlena Patricia Roriguez, Leslie the Amoeboid, and our sentient bodyguard and ally, Friday. My name is Tony, but I really call myself Fugitor."

"I'm Pamelyn. It's good to meet you all. Again I apologize for Sarah. You know how babies are, I'm sure."

"Believe me…I know." And I was right on that…but you didn't hear that from *me*.

And so, against my rather rush-about nature, and also much to the relief of my traveling comrades, we decided to spend a fair amount of Time in this Universe. With a great deal of reluctance on my part, I admitted that the rest would do me a, well, *world* of good.

During the course of our stay, Pamelyn informed us that in addition to her two-year-old daughter, she also had a seven-year-old son. I didn't think much about this at the time, but apparently she adopted both of them, first her son when she was just seventeen, and a year later she got her daughter…but not without a fight.

Presently Pamelyn turned 'round to me.

"Do you have a family, Tony?" she asked.

"Well…sad to say, no, I don't. See, I'm divorced, and I haven't any kids of my own, much as I adore them," I replied.

Marlena wondered about Pamelyn's son, the one I mentioned to you just now.

"Hey, Pamelyn, where *is* your son?" Marlena asked.

"Oh, David's asleep himself. He isn't feeling well now. Otherwise you'd be able to meet him." Pamelyn said this with a deal of sadness on her part.

"Oh, sorry to hear that," I said.

Soon the conversation got 'round to our adventures. Now *that* was a topic that I was more than a little reluctant to talk about to a young mother of two small children (in the age-wise sense of things), but again, not wishing to offend, I decided to forego myself and divulge everything (which you already know) up to this point…

CHAPTER TWENTY-ONE

Having related all my adventures to Pamelyn, we soon realized that the time for us to go was upon us. But before our leave-taking, we asked our kind and, I must admit, lovely hostess if we could at least *see* her son David.

Graciously, she led us to the bedroom, where we finally met her boy. He was slightly bigger than his sister, with thick brown hair, closed eyes that Pamelyn said were Celtic-blue in color, and was a little on the thin side. He wore a striped turtleneck shirt, brown trousers, and black socks. He was clearly asleep, only seldom stirring about. I had to admit, he was a good-looking lad. At least, that's what Marlena told me, anyway.

Finally, after the goodbyes were said, the four of us set off on our way. I really enjoyed myself, I must say, but I felt even gladder to be back on our sojourn once more.

Again, we bypassed star-system after star-system. Worlds beyond worlds, times beyond times; some in chaotic birth, others in their twilight and utter decline. By now, though, those sights had lost their wondrous luster…and it all grew quite -- I don't know -- *boring,* I felt.

And so, again it all fell into a now-bland routine. In the usual yet strange way, it was actually welcomed. I don't know about you, but right now we really *didn't* need any more weird excitement, thank you so much.

As is always ever the case, however, that feeling of ennui wouldn't endure for long.

Oh. I suppose you're wondering by now how we manage to get into these messes.

Well...to put it as basically and as bluntly as humanly possible, they find us!!

For you see, of all the strange and weirdly fascinating sights we'd encountered up till now, nothing—and I do mean—*nothing* could have ever prepared us for what undoubtedly was *the* most bizarre thing ever witnessed by all Humanity!!

In fact, it was so overwhelming that I can't begin to try to describe it as yet!

But...for the sake of those of you who have a stomach for weird stories such as this, well, I'll try to collect my thoughts together and do my damned best to talk about it.

Where to start? Hmmm…..okay.

For openers, it was a massively-wide spheroid, not unlike Leslie, only it was purely metallic; in fact, it was almost like a…floating Christmas ornament, with diamonds peppered about its form. Underneath it all was a shaft of some sort, though what its use was, I couldn't even dare make an off-the-wall guess. Again, I'd more than likely be off-target.

As we approached it for a closer study, we took note of the fact that we gazed at a group of shapes, humanoid in nature even though we didn't know what gender those shapes were at that state. The only reason we weren't all that certain was that, basically, they were too indistinct to tell for sure.

Suddenly, we turned 'round, courtesy of a warning signal from Friday.

"What is it, Friday?" I questioned.

"We've got to get out of here! NOW!!!"

"Why? What's wrong?" asked Marlena.

Instantly the "answer" came its way to us in the form of the most powerful tractor-beam imaginable!! Whoever was in that diamond-and-gold spheroid no doubt had spotted us!!

Before Marlena and Leslie could ask, I put forth some of my will-power in order to escape the beam's gravitational pull, and like before, the strain grew too much, and it began to show!

With that weary resignation, I relaxed my power, and thus we were on our way to yet another weird encounter…with an even weirder race!!

CHAPTER TWENTY-TWO

The moment we arrived inside the spheroid, a sense of awe and amazement washed over our frames. Even Friday, I must say, was truly impressed…again, if that's at all possible for a law-keeping fortress-ship to register such things!

"Hello? I say, is there anybody about?" I called out.

As we expected, a deafening silence permeated all about us. That is, for only a short spot of time, as we were to soon discover…

"Who enters here?" said a metallic yet clearly female voice.

"Oh, it's just us wayward time-space travelers, that's all," replied Marlena.

"Don't move an inch. Stay where you are. Please."

"Oh, okay. We're not going anywhere anyway," said Marlena.

I turned my gaze at Marlena.

"A little bit of advice: from now on, let *me* chat with beings like this, okay?" I said.

"It's your ball-game, Tony."

Time seemed to drag for what I thought were hours without end, though logically it was really 15 minutes, at that.

Then…a loud, droning clang met our ears, followed by a bright spotlight.

"Move into the light, strangers. Now."

We did as we were somewhat crassly instructed, and soon our "interrogator" made its—well, *her* way towards us.

She was a tall, golden, metallic female with bright red photo-optic eyes, perfectly white teeth -- don't ask, please -- and was rather on the well-chested side of her figure, which otherwise was slender. Her personality, however, left a lot ot be desired…like, say, better manners.

"Now… who are you strangers?" she asked, in her crass way.

Marlena was ready to answer, but knew now not to, so I did the replying.

"Hello. My name's Tony, alias Fugitor, and these three are my friends."

I made my way 'round the list, starting with, of course, Marlena, then Leslie, and finally Friday. If anything, the golden woman's demeanor grew even colder…which, with her shiny stature, seemed logical enough.

"All right, strangers…what brings you here?"

CHAPTER TWENTY-THREE

A surge of fear, such as we'd never felt before, crawled into our psyches as our alleged "hostess"

proceeded to thus question us in the most harshest way possible.

"Well? Aren't you going to answer me?!"

I tried to stall for time in order to respond.

"Well…" I began, "we'll answer your questions on one condition."

"Oh? And what's that?!" she asked prissily.

"Well, all I ask is that you show some form of elegance and grace in your manner. Is it a deal?" I

requested with some firm dignity.

The golden woman mulled over this for a few minutes.

"Oh, all right. I'll try, but I warn you, if you lie to me, I'll -- "

"Say no more. We've gotten the idea."

"Very well. Now...let's start over, huh? Where did you come from?"

"From beyond this Universe. In fact, as my friend Marlena pointed out, we come from beyond all Known Time and Space. I'm sure you can understand all that, can't you?"

She didn't reply at first. Evidently she was a little on the confused side of it all.

"I don't see why I really should, but I'll give you the benefit of a doubt, I suppose. Oh, before I forget my manners, allow me to introduce myself. My name's Hala. This is my vessel, the one that picked you up by pure dumb luck. And..." she said, with growing shame and humility, *"well, I'd like to apologize to you for how I am."*

We accepted her apology, and her interrogative manner slowly ebbed away.

"Excuse me, uh, Hala? How did you get so far out here in Space?" asked Marlena.

"Well, honey, it's a long story, so I hope you got time for it."

Seeing as how we weren't going anywhere for the moment, we decided to stick around and listen to her story.

"Well, as I just said, it's a really long story I've got to tell, so here goes. In answer to Marlena's question about why I'm so far out in Limitless Space, you can thank my ex-husband for that little idea. The jackass!!"

We grew quite stunned by *that* revelation, yet she carried on.

"Yeah, that's right. I was married, thanks to my manufacturers. See, I'm, or rather, was part of a wild marketing ploy to make robotics fit every aspect of Modern Life. Just think of it. Robots, like me, to do every known activity that Humans so take for granted...and much more."

While listening to all this, we tried our utmost best not to laugh, as implausible as it may sound to you or us.

(Well, I can wager by now that you're due to ask how all these weird characters relate these odd tales for all our collective benefit. I'll tell you at a later date, thank you.)

Getting back to Hala's tale…Marlena grew really *drawn* into the story being told now.

"Uh, Hala, when you said you were married, did you mean -- ?"

"Yeah, that's right, sweetheart. The minister, reception, ring, honeymoon, the whole nine yards."
Hala's anger seemed to mount, though we couldn't tell for certain.

"And, uh, did you, you know -- ?" asked Marlena further.

Hala paused tensely, as if deeply pained enough not to carry on.

"Yeah...we have two kids, a college-age son and a ten-year-old daughter. And if you want my advice, honey, don't *have kids. It ain't fun, believe me."*

"I say, Hala," I intejected, "not wishing to be rude or some such, but you said you were part of some odd marketing ploy or other."

Hala drew in a heavy breath -- at least, as heavy a breath as possible for an android.

"Oh, yeah, that's right. See, it was decided by our so-called 'duly-elected officials', such as that idiot 'King' Weigndin, to incorporate robots into the everyday community. Well, to make a long soap-opera-type story short for your benefit, a law was proposed, passed, and enacted in one fell swoop. Soon after, the race was on—and what *a race it was, believe me!*

"I was sent to the home of a former astronaut-turned-wealthy consultant, mostly to be a domestic. Well, you can figure out where that *led up to. We fell in love, got married, and I even got pregnant,* which is why we have our two kids. Yeah, *that's* hard to believe, huh?"

Leslie (whom I'd once more unintentionally neglected) turned 'round to Hala.

"*Say, before we got in here, we all noticed a group of blobs moving around,*" he said.

Hala snapped out of her morose state, and her demeanor improved slightly.

"*Oh, those. Just a group I picked up here and there. Mostly other robots, suddenly unemployed by the turbulent economic state of our planet. Ahh...that's life, I suppose.*"

"If your planet's economy is so shaky, then how did you afford this -- *thing?!*" asked Marlena, now insatiably curious by it all.

"*I didn't exactly* afford *it, honey. Basically, I stole it!!*"

Now we were in a truly shaken state!

"*You know, Hala, if you were in* my *Home Universe,*" boomed Friday, "*I'd have your lovely metallic keister in the can by now!! You, of all people, know that under Star-Guild Law-Code Section 38, paragraph 12, it clearly states, and I quote, 'All participants in theft of any sort is sub-*

jected to no less or not more than ten years in prison, or sentenced to twelve to twenty-four months in hard labor.' And I'm sure that hard labor won't do a thing for your figure. True?"

Hala now eyed Friday in a very intense manner, her ruby eyes blazing.

"Listen here, my fine Jack Webb sound-alike, your so-called 'Star-Guild' doesn't have any juris-diction here! I did what I did to survive! I'm not exactly thrilled about it! I have to live, don't I?" And with that, Hala almost ended any chance of future conversations, to put it mildly.

After we all collected ourselves, I made a diplomatic ploy, and decided to tell her what you already know by now, which is to say…just about everything.

Suddenly, that weird sensation had overtaken me, and I knew it was time for us to resumeour journey. This, I dismally realized to myself, is the one part I enjoy the least of all.

And so, we went up to Hala to say our farewells, and thanked her for her time. All out of good manners. Then, as usual, my resident walking light-bulb-minded lady-friend had one of her rather uncalled-for ideas.

To please Marlena, I proposed the idea to Hala.

"Thanks, but no. I've got my own destiny to fulfill. Plus, well, I'm due back home to see my kids…and just maybe I'll reconcile with my husband. I don't know just yet, though."

"Well, whatever way your path takes you, we do hope it all works out for the best for youand your family. I mean, we have seen *stranger* things happen, you know."

Just before we departed, we thought we caught a glimpse of a tear or two rolling down Hala's lovely yet clearly saddened face.

Well…onwards and onwards once more.

And this time, I had a date…with Justice!

CHAPTER TWENTY-FOUR

"Say, Tony, may I ask you something?"

This is what Friday asked me moments after our newest departure.

"Sure, Friday. What's on your mind?"

He paused, while Leslie and Marlena looked on.

"You didn't think I was too rough on Hala, did you?"

I paused for only a short spell.

"Well…maybe a tad rough there, Friday. Just a bit."

"Yeah, maybe I do come off as a bit rough, but that's sort of my nature. You understand that,

right?"

Not surprisingly, I did understand. And I think Friday knew that, because he never seemed to get

all down about it all.

Leslie and Marlena got onto a new subject.

"Uh, Tony, you have any idea where we're going to next?" asked Leslie, with a dash of concern

on his part.

"Yeah, that's right, huh? Where *are* we going?" added Marlena.

I thought it was high time that I reveal the truth to my friends…but not right away. See, I wanted

more than ever to destroy my former masters once and for all, though, as I'm sure I stated many

times throughout, I had no desire to place their lives in danger just out of my admittedly selfish

wish for Vengeance.

I grew to learn a lot about Life itself during the course of it all, and what I did learn, well, I can't dare say that it wasn't the least bit exciting!!

And what *did* I learn, you're no doubt asking?

Well...that's a rather tricky if not difficult question to respond to, so for now do let's leave off trying, thanks.

And so, with little else to discuss, our sojourn dragged on and on. The tedium bore down on us, and inside our psyches a growing irritation gnawed about us, though we dared not show it to one another lest we irreparably destroyed the staunch friendship we were justly proud to display for all to notice.

Finally...the time had arrived for me to reveal the truth. Now.

I turned 'round to my friends, albeit somberly.

Marlena and Leslie read that said somber look on my face. They somehow knew.

I made my plans be known.

"Marlena…Friday…Leslie. It's Truth or Consequences time. Our next destination is…my Home World. I have a rather dour plot in my mind. And I wish you to know now that you don't have to go along with me, if that's your desire.

"See, what I'm about to execute could, rightly so, put your lives in grave danger, so if you wish me to take you back to your home Universes, say so now and I'll do my jolly best to grant you requests. Is that satisfactory for you lot?"

Not one of my fellow Space-Time travellers uttered a word. I sensed that they were pondering what I had just revealed.

The moment of truth on their part came by way of Marlena.

"Tony…the three of us thought it over…and we'd like to say…well, we'll stay with you all the way through this thing." She was supremely if somewhat foolishly confident in her declaration.

I didn't believe what I heard!

"Uh, maybe you weren't quite paying attention to what I had told you. Your lives could be in utter and total Danger!! I just can't have that on my conscience. I just can't!"

"You're forgetting one thing, Tony." That came from Friday.

"Oh? What's that?" I asked, with more than a little bit of surprise.

"You have me. Maybe you just temporarily didn't remember how powerful I can get in times of trouble. But I guess that's understandable, with all that's happened to you up to this point. That's why you have us as friends. To get you through these times, if you'll excuse the term so loosely used."

"Besides…you can't for certain be in *that* much of a hurry, can you?" asked Marlena.

She had a point. Inwardly I thought that Justice can wait just a smidgeon longer. That was a good thing for me, because another moment of truth had come my way. And I knew that it had to do with my true feelings for Marlena, based on the advice Leslie gave me much, much, *much* earlier in our voyages.

Presently I turned my gaze 'round to her.

"Marlena…there's something I had been meaning to say to you, but with so much going on, well, quite frankly, I didn't get an opportune chance to tell you."

She looked at me in quite a perplexed manner.

"Uhh…okay. What is it?" she queried.

I gulped audibly.

This was *it!!*

"Marlena…I want to say…well—how am I to say this?—Marlena, I -- " I said, my voice slightly faltering.

"Oh, Tony," she said, smiling. "I already know."

And with that said, she and I embraced one another tightly, not noticing Leslie and Friday about us. We simply just didn't care.

Then…she planted the most intense, passionate kiss on my lips. Now we two truly became as one…and we did indeed welcome it!

No more now need be said. It is what it is, I suppose….

CHAPTER TWENTY-FIVE

With my love for Marlena, and hers for me, now declared and confirmed, we soon set ourselves about the task of executing my plan to take out my former masters-turned archenemies, which had been still formulating in the deepest recesses of my mind.

However, that plan was to be delayed by yet another weird encounter!

For just then, into our line of vision was undoubtedly the *oddest* sight imaginable!!

Imagine, if you can try to, a vessel resembling nothing less than a gigantic cheeseburger, complete with the fixings, namely catsup, mustard, lettuce, onions, and even an olive planted firmly on top via a toothpick.

It was all we did to keep from laughing at just such a sight as this!!

What occurred next, well -- just see for yourself:

"Hey, I don't bite, unless you bite first. Come on in," called out a voice emanating from the floating cheeseburger itself!!

With nothing to lose except our manners, we made our way to the burger which, in actuality, was another fortress-ship, not unlike Friday in dimensions if not overall demeanor. In fact, I was starting to suspect if Friday had some relatives he apparently knew nothing about. Naturally, I didn't broach up on the subject, as it was really none of my personal affair, anyway.

Having just entered the floating fortress-ship, we gazed 'round inside the interior,and took notice of the fact that ouside of a few pieces of basic if somewhat advanced (by our standards) machinery, it was otherwise totally empty. And yet our curiosity grew exponentially, as is the usual case in these weird circumstances. Such is the way, I suppose.

"Hello?" I shouted. "I say, is there anybody about?"

"About what?" called out the ship's voice, in a strange reply.

I had no time for these stupid, almost idiotically childish games. And I said so.

"Look, whoever you are, do come on out and talk to us. We mean you no harm."

Instantly a *whirring* sound greeted our ears, and we knew that it was a compartment door opening up. Then…what appeared to be a mobile box-shaped roundabout, like a shipping-crate on wheels, motored its way to our position, just only stopping near-directly my toes.

"Okay, here I come," said that eccentric voice.

A side-panel on the roundabout opened, and outside it stepped a tall, bespectacled man with curly blond hair. He was wearing a rather mundane three-piece suit, greyish in color, with accesorily black shoes.

"Well, I'm out!" he stated, thrusting his arms out like a comedic showman of sorts.

This struck Marlena as so funny, she laughed herself silly for at least ten minutes.

As usual, my patience rapidly ran itself out.

"Oh, do stop carrying on so!" I said to her angrily.

She tried, and failed, to stop laughing.

"Oh, I'm sorry, Tony. It's just that--" she uttered, then resumed laughing again.

Presently I turned 'round to the tall businessman.

"You're not--?" I stammered.

"Yeah, I get that a lot, huh? Well, you know how it is," he replied. "Oh, I'm Arthur Landesberg, by the way. Saw you flying around out there, and decided to pick you up."

"Thank you so kindly," I replied.

And in a quick flash of time I made the usual courteous introductions, starting off with my sniggering girlfriend, then Leslie, and at last Friday.

"Glad to meet you. Say," Arthur said, pointing at Marlena,"what's with her?"

In reply, I gazed back at her. She finally stopped her hideous guffaw-session.

"Well?" I asked her, twinged with a dash of irritation.

"Oh, I'm sorry again," she replied. "It's just that when you said, 'I'm out' in the way you showed, I thought that, well, you know--"

"Oh, that. Yeah. I get *that* a lot, too. Well, actually, I'm married, or was, anyway."

A weird and somewhat obvious connection registered itself in my mind.

"I say, Arthur, I don't want to be crass about this subject, but you weren't, by any strange chance, married to a woman named...Hala, were you?" I asked, trying to not offend our host.

"Oh, you mean the robot girl," he responded, nonchalantly.

Our jaws dropped in utter amazement.

"How did you -- ?" stammered Marlena, her eyes bulging about.

"Near as I can tell, everyone knows about her. Nope, wasn't married to her, though. My wife's name's Liz. I don't go in for those artificial types. Too high-strung, I think." During the course of our conversation, he perpetually flashed a rather smug smile, which made it difficult to take him seriously. But I suppose that was part of his charming if slightly off-the-wall way.

Well…as is the usual case by now, we once more related our increasingly long and unbelievable tale in regards to our voyages and experiences up to our current point. To our total surprise, he didn't seem to be all that impressed. I guess that he'd just about seen it all.

Unexpectedly, the conversation grew 'round to our immediate future plans.

I didn't wish to answer his questions, as I felt that those immediate plans I just mentioned to you were extremely personal, so to make a long story short for your benefit, I merely stated to Arthur that our futures were of the long-overdue persuasion, and that they definitely *needed* to be taken care of. This satisfied him...but he then had a sudden request.

"Say, Tony, you mind if I tag along? I get awfully bored just living in this Digital-Age metal cheeseburger. Besides...it's 'pickling' my brain, if you get my drift."

To my chagrin, Marlena and Leslie *both* started laughing in the most uproariously annoying way possible. If anything, I actually, and literally, felt steam buzzing out my ears.

Looking at Friday helplessly, I shook my head in dismay.

"Sorry, son, can't help you there," he said.

I nodded my head in agreement.

Leslie floated his way 'round to me.

"Hey, Tony, you gotta love *this guy!! He's GREAT!!"* he chortled loudly.

Ignoring this laugh-festival as diplomatically as I can muster(no cheap Arthur-inspired pun in-tended, I assure you), I made my point be quite clearly known.

"If we can, let's carry on with the leave-taking, shall we?"

"Yeah. Take-out. You know," quipped Arthur, that wacky grin ever present.

And as is usual anymore, my stomach churned at this one, I can tell you now…

CHAPTER TWENTY-SIX

After the preparations and provisions were set, we left Arthur's former home and soon we found once more journeying through worlds beyond worlds, times beyond times; only now, I, myself personally, was now utterly rady and more than willing to return to my home world and at last face them in the showdown that had been long in coming!!

And in fact, in a sense, it was *our* fight, as well. I felt a real elation as I grew ever so grateful for Leslie, Friday, our new friend Arthur Landesberg, and the love of my life, Marlena. Yet I couldn't help but house the lingering thought in my mind about the outcome of this upcoming war. It's as though…we were only bit players in some Grand Cosmic Scheme, but as yet I didn't know who was concocting this plot. I mean, I'm not prone to any sort of religious belief or cosmological superstition, but it made me wonder. And I had no doubt in my mind, as I'm sure I told the others, that their lives were in grave danger. But…that's par for the course, I suppose.

I mulled over these new thoughts for a long while, not really up for idle chat.

Just then, Marlena turned about to me.

"Tony? You okay? What's wrong?"

I didn't answer right away. This was *one* time I really needed to think.

"Oh…just doing a lot of thinking, that's all."

She looked at me warily and sadly. I suspected that she knew…about it all. But she didn't let on about it. I had to hand it to her, she was a strong young woman, and as I said, I was glad to have her with me during the duration of this adventure.

Then, my reverie was interrupted by Friday's warning beacon.

"We're almost there, Tony."

"Thanks, Friday," I meekly replied.

I didn't mention this, but I felt my courage falter for the first time ever. But I had made my resolve, and I was to carry it out—to the *bitter* end, if necessary.

Another signal informed us that we'd just entered the orbital field of my former home planet.

We thus gritted our teeth grimly, aware of the ensuing battle that now grew distinct in our psyches. And...those dark thoughts in my mind grew more and more consuming!!

I knew, for *all* our sakes, that I had to put them aside.

The time for war was *on!!*

CHAPTER TWENTY-SEVEN

We landed outside the Bureacracy's HQ Building, just a mere mile from the heart of the pestilence that, while pretending to be "pious" had in actuality brought turmoil, strife, and misery to those having the misfortune of falling under their spell of lies!

For long hour after hour we scoped out any means of access without being detected.

"I say, Friday, would you do the service of scanning, please?"

"It'll be my pleasure, Tony." And with that, Friday set off doing his thing which, to my sheer amazed delight, he was a true master of.

Within a few minutes, he came back with the results.

"Well...the best I can tell you is to have you climb up the building's left side, and there you should find an air-shaft leading into the Bureaucracy's center. It isn't that high, so you shouldn't

have too much trouble getting in." Then he added, *"It's getting* out *that's going to be tricky."* He sounded almost fearful, and I can understand that.

Putting *that* little bit of news aside, we proceeded to do as instructed.

An hour later we emerged in the very sick heart of the Bureaucracy itself. We four, namely myself, Leslie, Marlena, and Arthur, just looked 'round the perimeter, expecting the proverbial other shoe to drop.

We sweated out the moments, in my case literally.

The tension from waiting ate us up alive.

And then --

Aha!! As I expected!

A bright light activated itself suddenly, and there before our very eyes, stood the inhuman and in-humane machinery that is the Bureaucracy. Now, I couldn't tell for certain, but evidently they were most displeased to see me again.

"So, FGTR-5183, we see you've decided to join us again," said the Head One.

"Like hell!!" I snarled, a sly grin on my face. "And my name is either Tony or Fugitor. Do try to use either one, huh?!"

The Head One got to the point.

"You have disobeyed us for the final time, Fugitor. Your Eternal Exile now will be nothing com-pared to the destruction you will now face. Now...did you honestly think *that you, of all carbo-noids, could actually set out and ruin our plans?!"*

"I don't have to think about that. I just plan to *do* it!!!" I sneered, that sly grin intact.

The Head One paused somewhat ruefully.

"You are a brave man, Fugitor, we'll say that *for you. But your bravery is foolish at best, and at worst it is useless. Now…"* the Head One said, *"you have two choices. Rejoin our cause, or… DIE!! Decide now!!"*

It didn't even take me a milli-second to reply.

"Well, I decided."

"And?" asked the Head One.

"It's death…for you, you---*bastards!!!!"*

A tense silence permeated all about.

"So be it, my friend. So be *it!!"*

Now it was truly on!!

(All while this was going on, unbeknownst to me, Marlena and Arthur somehow or other found their way into the Communications sector, and re-wired the intercoms to directly link up with Friday, with Leslie inside the gallant fortress-ship's structure. The Head One, then, was in for one hell of a rude surprise!!)

"Friday!! Now!!!" I shouted as loudly as I could.

"What's the meaning of this ploy, Fugitor?"

In reply to the Head One's question, a barrage of salvos from Friday's weapon systems shook the very building intensely, as though a massive earthquake had struck!! A few minutes afterwards, Leslie floated his way to me.

"Uh, I do hope I'm not late for the party," he said.

I smiled at that quip.

"No, you're right on time, old friend!" I cheered joyously.

Instantly Leslie made his to one Bureaucracy computer after another, literally *sliming* the SOBs; in fact, so much so that quickly each machine shorted itself out completely and beyond repair!! Boy, I'd hate to see *that* bill.

Now it was Marlena's chance, and she wasted no time at all. In a flash, she raced 'round to the secondary units, and performed the greatest act of heroic sabotage I had ever witnessed. Console after console was now ripped to shreds, as my love pulled out every wire imaginable.

She was about to make her way to the Head One, but I stopped her.

"No, Marlena…this bastard's all *mine!!!*"

Gary Cooper, eat your heart out!!

CHAPTER TWENTY-EIGHT

There we stood, eyeing one another like rival gunfighters in the Old West (not that I'm a fan of cowboy movies, you do understand). It's as if all Time literally slowed itself down in cold, slow anticipation of the first move…

The Head One's periscopic cobra-like eye swung its way 'round to me, studying and searching for any sign of hesitation on my part.

None would be forthcoming, much to his disappointment. My resolve held staunch.

"Best surrender now, Fugitor. It's the one true *way of the Universe. Things such as 'resolve', 'hope', and 'freedom' are mere illusions in the poor, deluded minds of the carbonoids known collectively as Man. They're utterly useless in the Grand Scheme of things. You, with your gitfted intellect, of all people should truly realize that."*

I, of course, didn't pay the Head One any mind. I think this irritated him more than anything by this stage.

Instantly a rather weird thought entered into my mind. What it actually *was,* well, I couldn't

place my creative finger on it as of yet. But by instinct, I knew that it would undoubtedly be the

most . . . I don't know -- *dynamic* one ever.

Unbeknownst to me, ever-reliable Leslie made his way toward the Head One and made the at-

tempt to slime the SOB.

What happened next set off the utmost cataclysmic chain of events.

For you see --well, you'll have to look...and try not to depress yourself.

"Anyone for a lube job?" he uttered. *"Free of charge."*

See, Leslie didn't realize that the Head One came all-too-prepared for everything that came his

way.

He -- Leslie, that is--was ready to slime him.

Then…

"*EYAAAAAAHHH!!!!*" screamed my amoeboid-friend in pain.

What happened was that the Head One activated a special laser that droned itself from the periscope-eye, literally *freezing Leslie on contact!!* Leslie never knew what hit him.

Forgetting my showdown for the nonce, I raced to my friend, as did Marlena and Arthur. And the tears rolled down our faces!

It was a morbidly traumatic sight, seeing our friend crystallised and lifeless. And yet, in the deep recesses of my mind, I felt his sacrifice wasn't at all in vain.

Slowly, like an automaton, I made my way back to the Head One, my grey-blue eyes nowlike cold fire blazing.

I casually grabbed his periscope-eye, and with a strength laced with latent insanity I ripped it out from his base-frame.

"What are you doing? What is this you do?" he asked. He'd get no reply.

In an instant, I swung the now-useless eye 'round and 'round, striking him with each step. The fear from the Head One grew qutie distinct by now.

"NO!! Wait!!! Please!! Mercy!!!" he pleaded.

Mercy, he said. I didn't show him any at all. I mean, why should I?

Soon after that, I dove into him like a madman, just ripping pieces out of him as though I were a careless surgeon.

Behind me, Marlena and Arthur just stood in awe at the sight they now witnessed.

Then…I found the very bloody heart of the Head One himself. Now his piteous cries for mercy and forgiveness intensified!

"Please!! PLEASE!!!! I was only doing my job!! No more!!!!"

Again, I didn't show one sign of granting his request. My nice-bloke demeanor had gonefrom me completely. No one would *dare* stop me from my wrath now!!

As I was about to make the final move, something stayed my hand…and that "something"came in the form of the most *intense* light imaginable, even as a friendly voice called out to me!!

"All right, Tony. You've made your point. Now that's enough."

I whirled 'round, and there before my very eyes stood a medium-height man in what appeared to be United States Army fatigues, olive-green in color, with complimentary black lace-up boots. He had salt-and-pepper hair with matching mustache. He seemed to emanate a sense of serene calm, as his slight smile demonstrated.

"Who are you?" I asked.

"Hi, Tony. My name's Sidney. I'm one of the Fates of Time."

I couldn't, or rather, *wouldn't* believe it!

"The Fates of Time, you said? I thought they were only a legend, or at least--"

"Something out of a science fiction tale, right? Well, I'm as real as I get, Tony. Now...why were you going to rip the Head One's heart out?"

I don't quite know why I answered this guy, but I did regardless.

"It's simple. He represents hopelessness and failure. He represents the destruction of Mankind's dreams and aspirations. And that, I dare *not* tolerate, thank you very much."

Sidney waltzed his way up to me.

"Follow me, Tony." He turned to my two remaining living companions. *"You, too, Marlena and Arthur. Come along. Don't be chicken."*

"Actually, I'm more of a cheeseburger guy myself. Lived in one, you know," said Arthur in that

copyrighted nonchalant manner of his.

CHAPTER TWENTY-NINE

Having just done as Sidney instructed, we turned our gazes 'round to him intently.

"All right, Sidney," I said, "now what?"

He didn't miss a step, this Sidney fellow. A strange man indeed…

"Well, now you just relax and listen to my explanation."

We did so. I mean, we weren't going anywhere at that stage.

"You see, everything that's happened to you up until now was according to the New and Noble Destiny we have in store for you."

"New and Noble Destiny?" questioned Marlena.

"That's right, Marlena. It's going to be your assigned task to root out all Injustice, no matter what form it takes. It can come in the shape of a creature, a man, in your case a machine, or even an Idea. And let me tell you now, folks, Ideas are the hardest *forms of Injustice to destroy!"*
Sidney grew slightly pained as he related all these to us.

"Wow. So in other words, it's 'bad Idea', huh?" quipped Arthur.

"Well, you could say that, I suppose. Now...are you all in this?"

We hesitated in our response. I mean, this was no easy decision. And where would Friday fit in this New and Noble Destiny, I found myself wondering.

Sensing all this somehow, Sidney replied to my thought.

"Oh, I wouldn't worry about Friday. He's part of the new Grand Scheme, too. Only his *Destiny lies within his programming."*

"So in other words -- ?" said Marlena.

"Sad to say, Friday's going back to his own Universe. His job's not done yet." Sidney turned his gaze skyward. *"So what do you say, Friday? You ready to get the bad guys?"*

"Yeah, I'm ready, Sidney. Mind if I say goodbye to my friends first?" asked Friday.

Sidney granted his request, and thus Friday delivered his farewells. Within a few secondsof doing this, the mighty yet noble fortress-ship sped off…never to return.

"Now…shall we be getting on our way, team? There's a lot of work to do, and my fellow Fates of Time need all the help they can get. How about it?"

We three turned and looked 'round at one another. And decided.

"Sure. Why not?" I said.

"I'll go only if I get to be with Tony," replied Marlena.

"Yeah, what the hell. I'll 'relish' this," quipped Arthur in deference to his fast-food home in Space. He seemed glad about it all.

And as for Marlena and myself in regards to the future, well—I can't say.

That, I dare say, is for another time….

AUTHOR'S AFTERWORD

In a way, this is my second "collaboration" with the English rock group Genesis, so I guess the first thing to do is personally thank their keyboardist Tony Banks, for serving as the inspiration behind(and literal model for)this story. I'm sure that if he were reading this, he'd deeply appreciate it.

Second, I'd like to dedicate these words to:

LESLIE NIELSEN

(1926-2010)

STEVE LANDESBERG

(1945-2010)

Thirdly, I'd like, of course, to deeply and truly thank the following masters of creativity who, in their own "weird manner"(as Fugitor says), have guided me along: Michael Moorcock, Roy Huggins, Jack Webb, and Larry Gelbart. Then lastly, I owe a good deal of thanks to the National Geographic Society, in particular the editors of the *National Geographic* magazine from the September, 1978 issue, for providing the lovely visual inspiration for Marlena.

Oh! Before I forget, I want to thank my friend Henry Seymour III, for helping to keep my eyes on the prize. Thanks for it all, buddy!

And, of course, to my fellow SF/fantasy fans, keep the wonder alive!!

Sincerely yours,

Thomas R. Skidmore

Western Pennsylvania

December 27, 2010

AUTHOR'S UPDATE

Just so you all know, this is the revised edition of *Fugitor: The Time Escapee* that I set about cleaning up and polishing. I mainly did this out of a sense of editorial concerns if not a sense of perfectionism as far as my writing goes. In other words, I wanted this to look and sound right to the readers' collective minds' eyes.

Now, I know it's a pain to revisit one's earlier works but in my case, again it's out of necessity. Plus it's a good way for me, as a writer, to learn the tricks of the trade in order to help me grow as an author, an editor, and as a person.

Lesson learned, you ask?

That's all on you, people.

Thomas R. Skidmore

Pittsburgh, PA

February 3, 2013

Made in the USA
Columbia, SC
23 November 2022

71976471R00211